HAPPY SPARK DAY!

ALADDIN New York · London · Toronto · Sydney · New Delhi

DRAGONS OF EMBER CITY

HAPPY SPARK DAY!

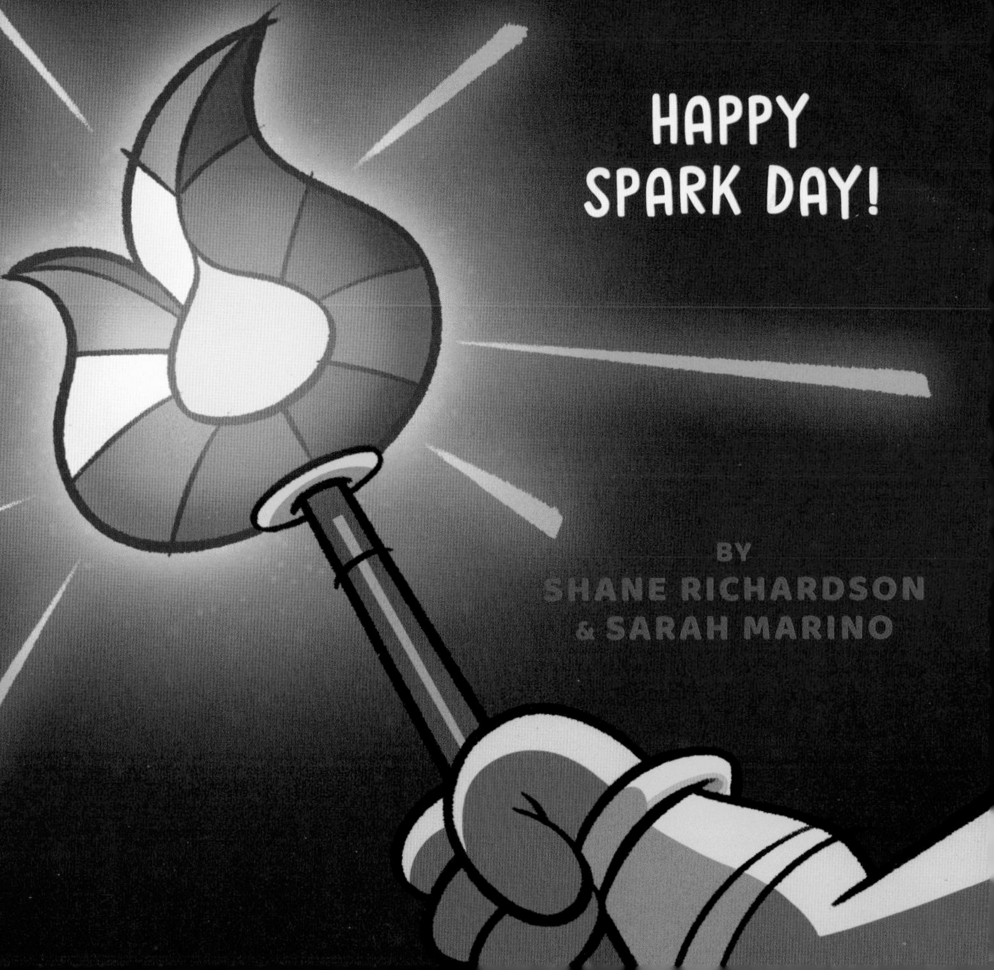

BY
SHANE RICHARDSON
& SARAH MARINO

ALADDIN

An imprint of Simon & Schuster Children's Publishing Division
1230 Avenue of the Americas, New York, New York 10020
First Aladdin edition October 2022
Copyright © 2022 by Shane Richardson and Sarah Marino
All rights reserved, including the right of reproduction in whole or in part in any form.
ALADDIN and related logo are registered trademarks of Simon & Schuster, Inc.
For information about special discounts for bulk purchases, please contact
Simon & Schuster Special Sales at 1-866-506-1949 or business@simonandschuster.com.
The Simon & Schuster Speakers Bureau can bring authors to your live event. For more information or to book an event contact the Simon & Schuster Speakers Bureau at
1-866-248-3049 or visit our website at www.simonspeakers.com.
Designed by Laura Lyn DiSiena
The illustrations for this book were rendered digitally.
The text of this book was set in FS Me and Kabouter.
Manufactured in China 0622 SCP
2 4 6 8 10 9 7 5 3 1
Library of Congress Control Number 2022933818
ISBN 9781534475243 (hc)
ISBN 9781534475236 (pbk)
ISBN 9781534475250 (ebook)

To our families—
for always believing in our Sparks
—Shane & Sarah

CHAPTER ONE

It was a special day in Ember City,
land of the dragons.
Young dragons everywhere would
find out what their Spark was.

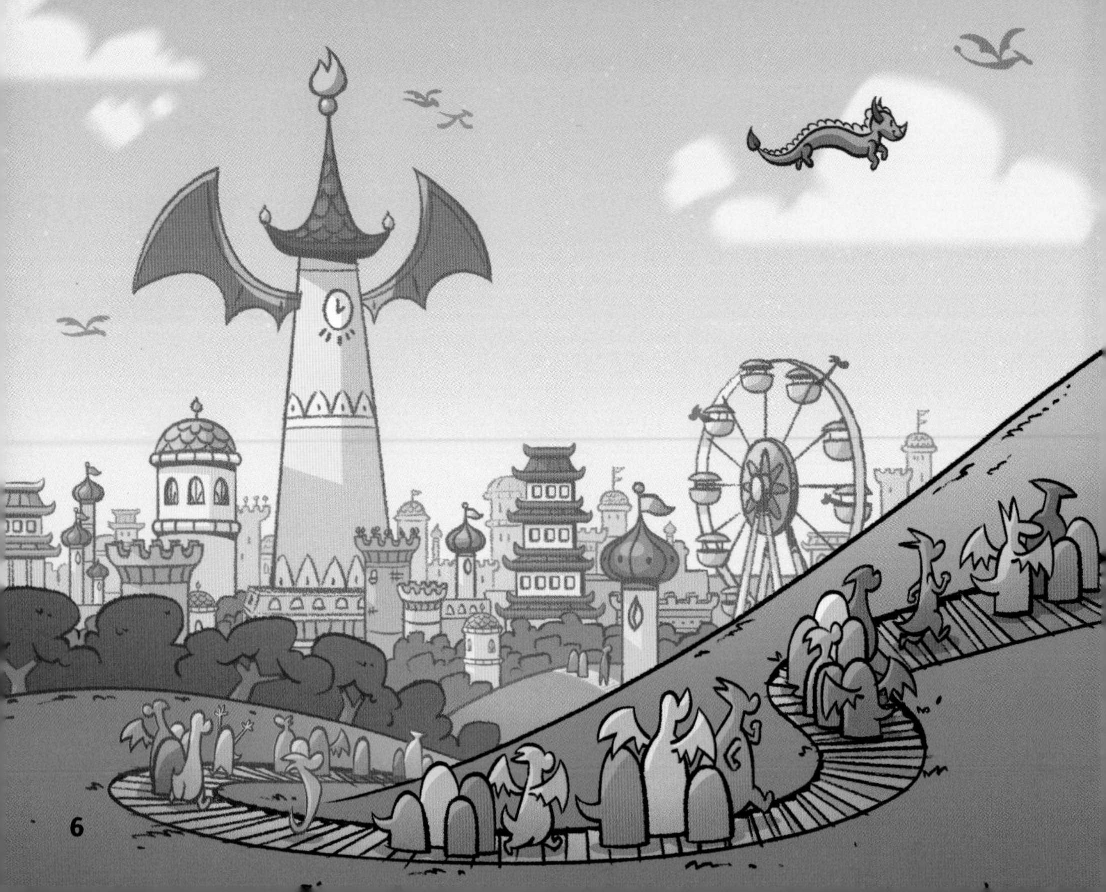

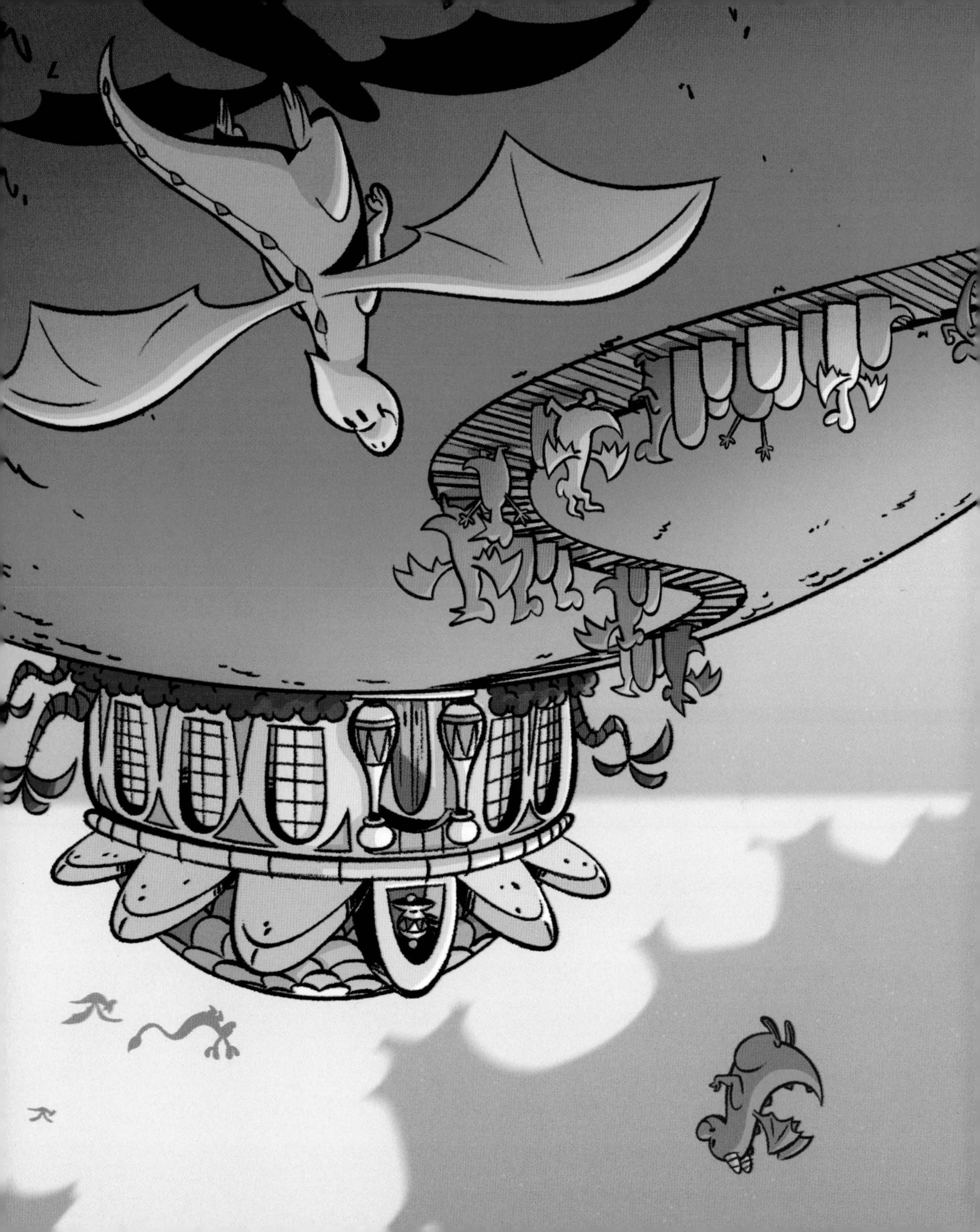

What’s a Spark? It’s a unique power granted by the Ember Stone.

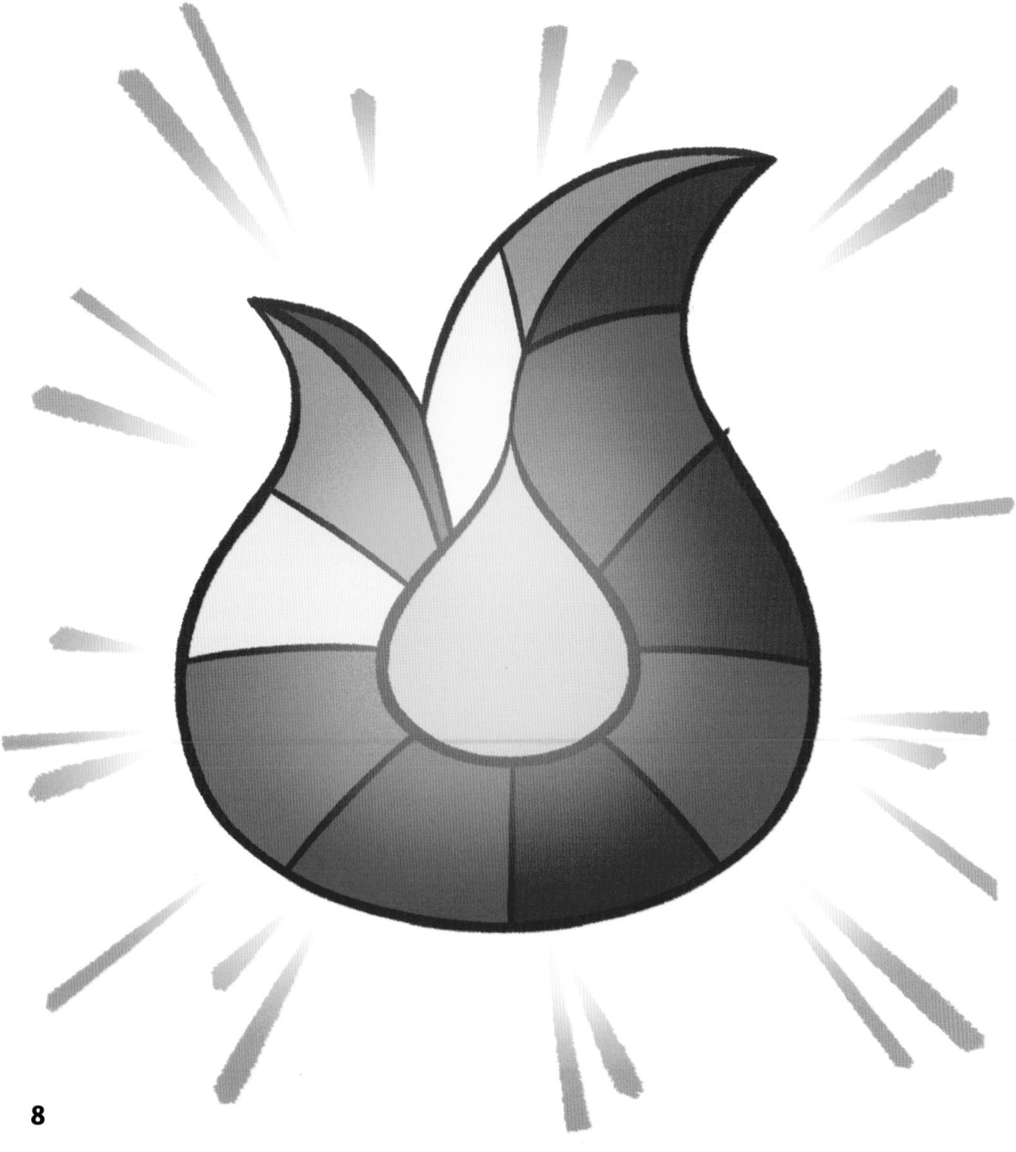

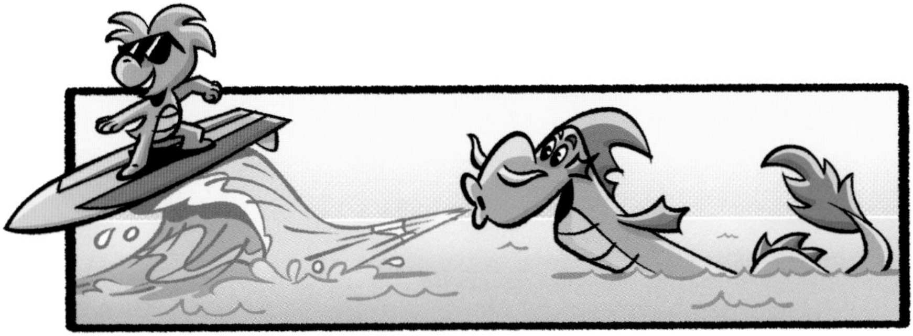

Some Sparks could be super strong, like a Water Spark!

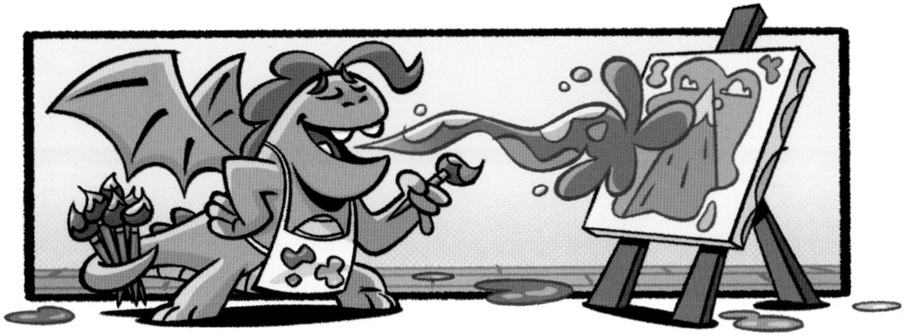

Some Sparks could be super fun, like a Paint Spark!

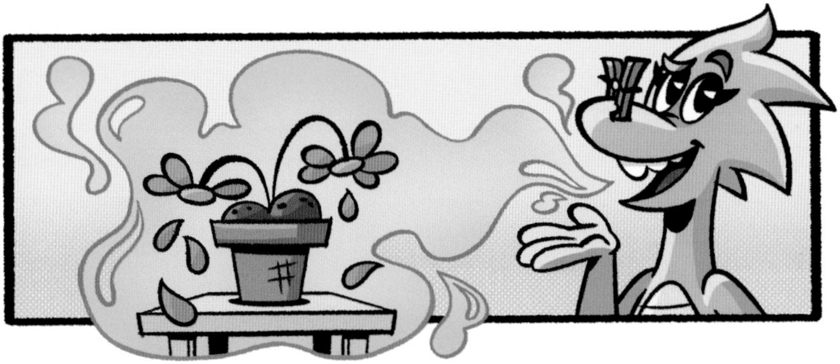

And some Sparks could even be super silly,
like a Stinky Spark!

But all Sparks had to be used wisely.

Today Drake, Runa, and Li, the best of dragon friends, would receive their magical powers.

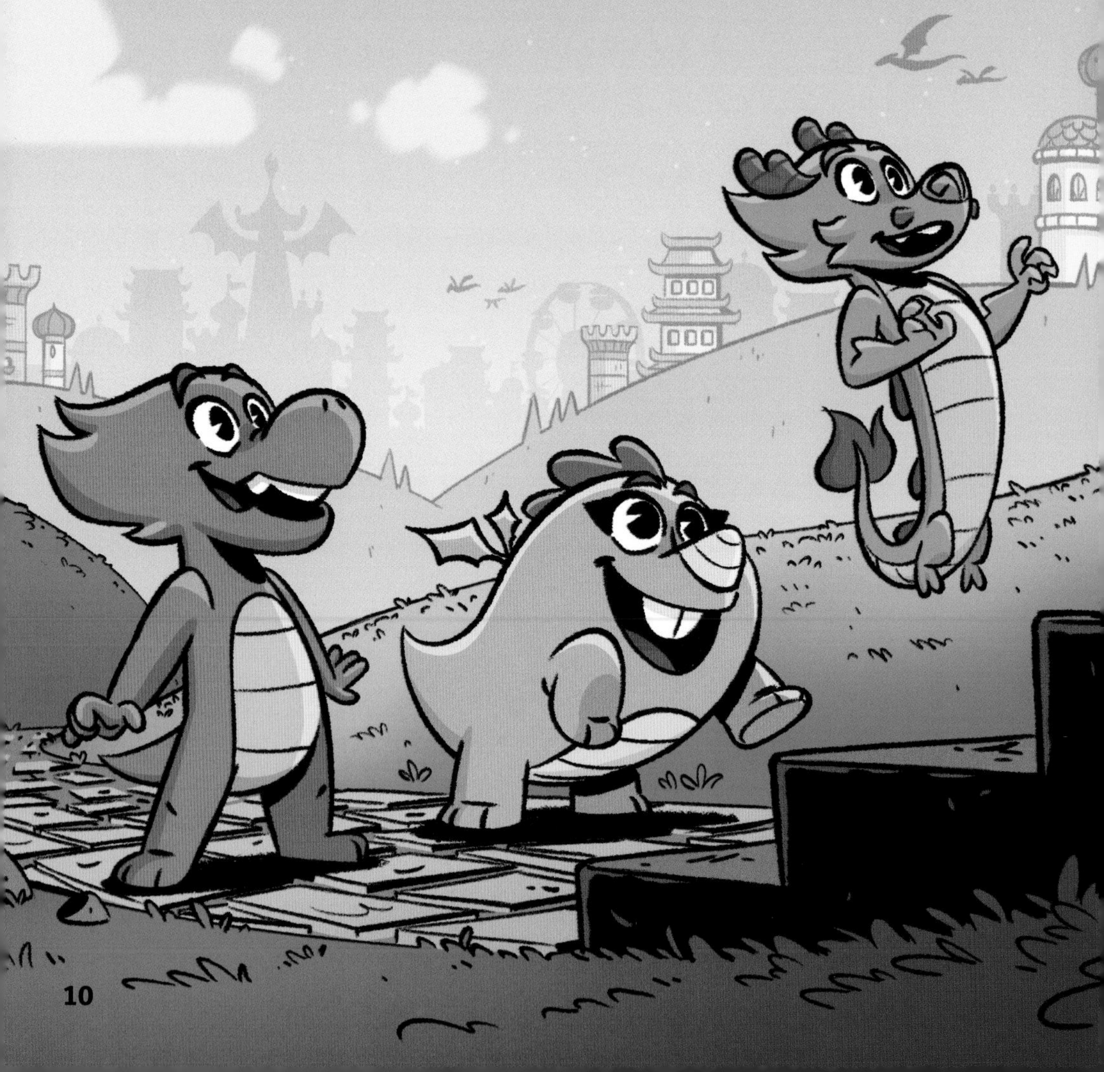

LI

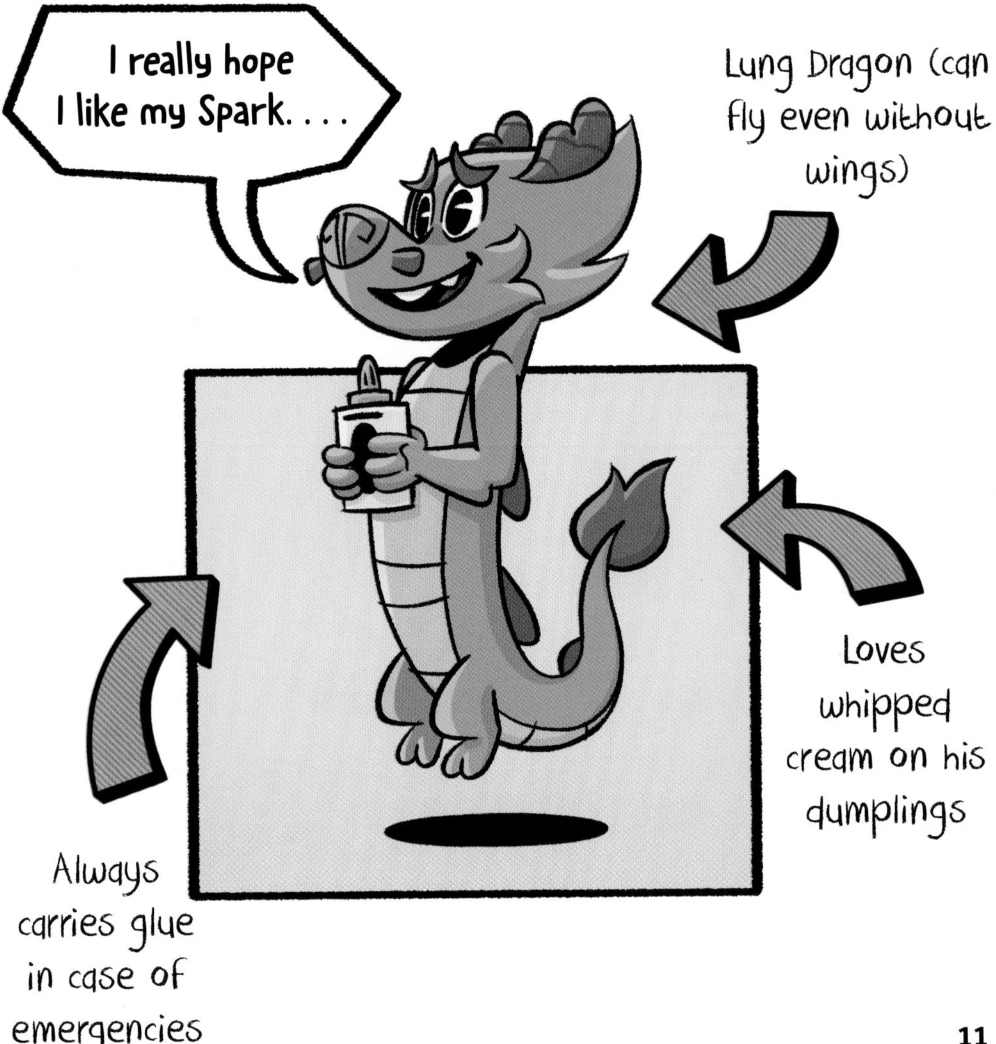
I really hope I like my Spark. . . .
Lung Dragon (can fly even without wings)
Loves whipped cream on his dumplings
Always carries glue in case of emergencies

RUNA

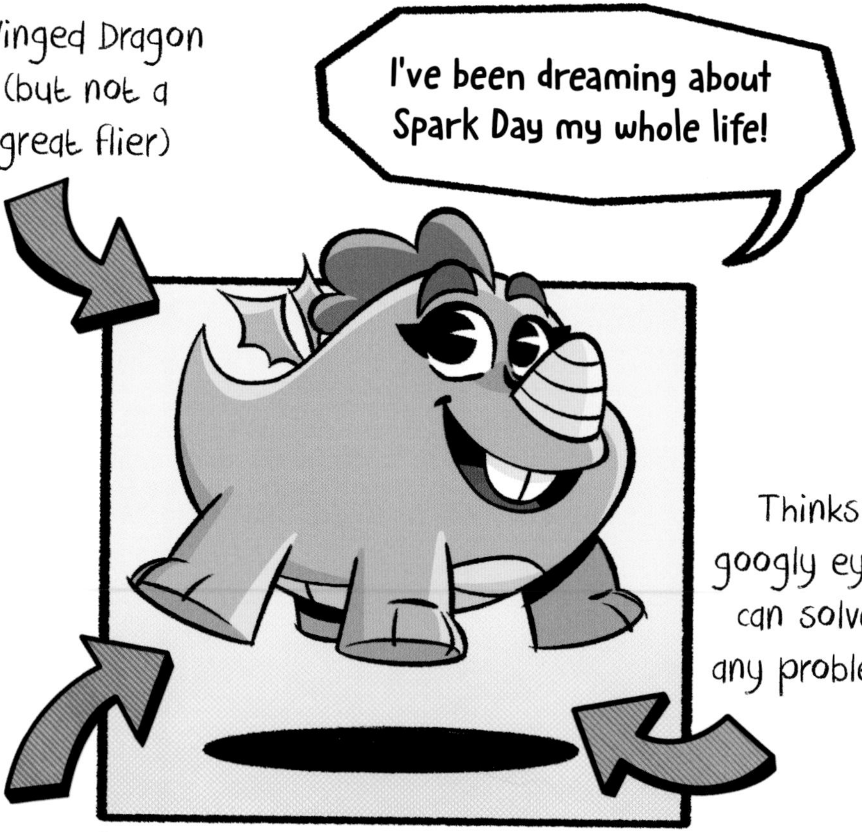
Winged Dragon (but not a great flier)
I've been dreaming about Spark Day my whole life!
Thinks googly eyes can solve any problem
Has a unicorn plushy collection

DRAKE

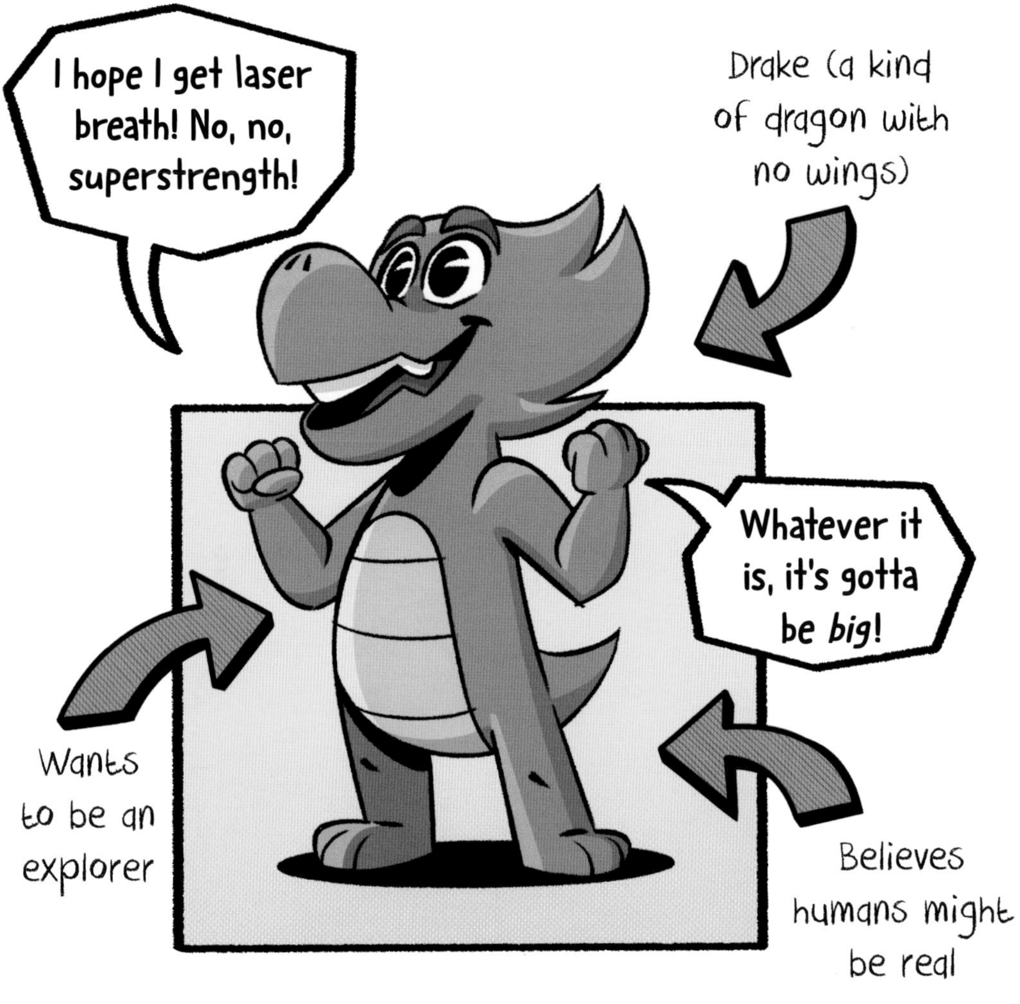
I hope I get laser breath! No, no, superstrength!
Drake (a kind of dragon with no wings)
Whatever it is, it's gotta be *big*!
Wants to be an explorer
Believes humans might be real

And this was **FIZZ**.

He and Drake didn't always see eye to eye.

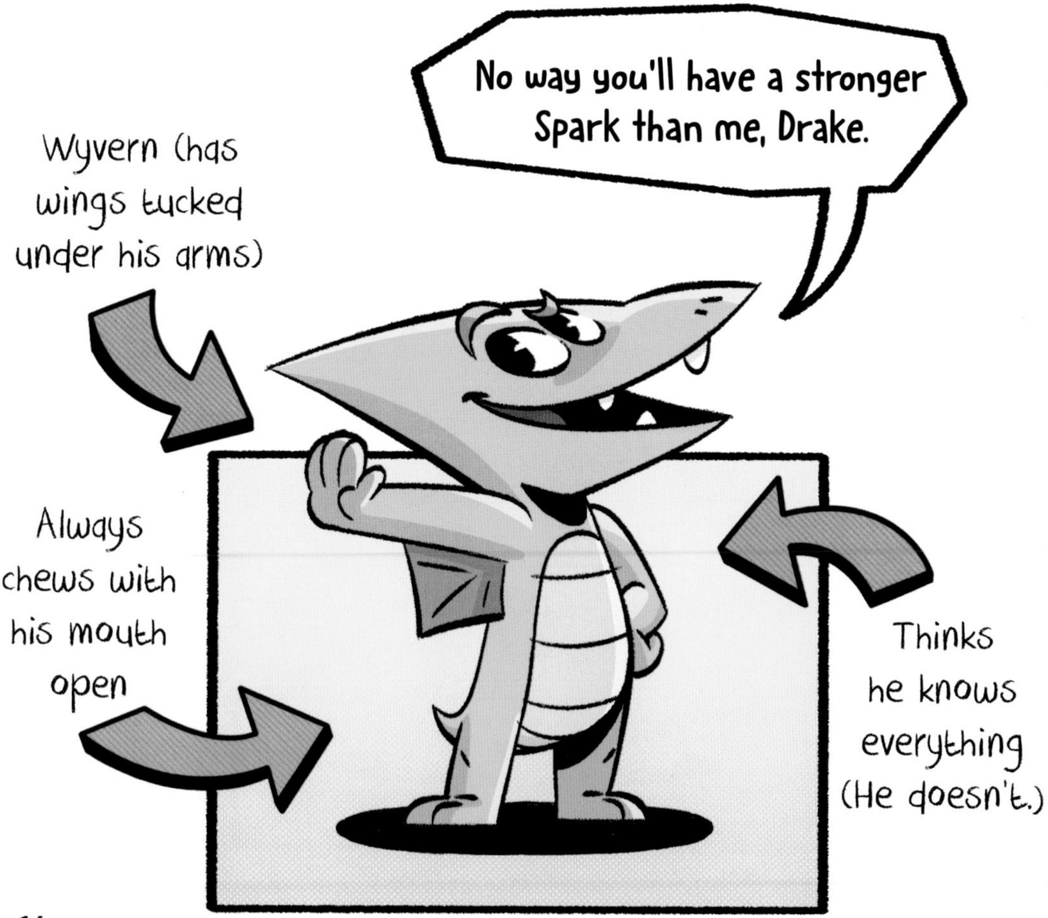
No way you'll have a stronger Spark than me, Drake.
Wyvern (has wings tucked under his arms)
Always chews with his mouth open
Thinks he knows everything (He doesn't.)

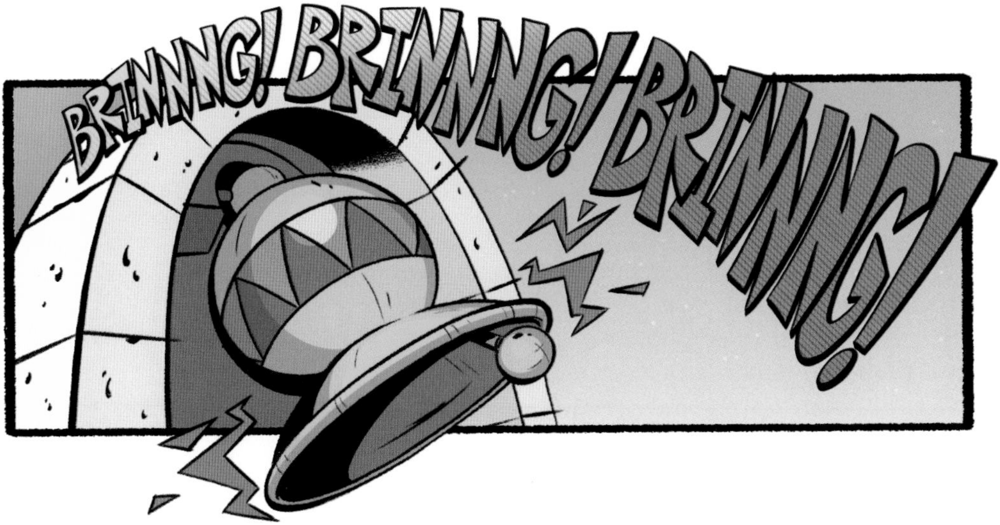
BRINNNG! BRINNNG! BRINNNG!

Three rings of the Ember Theater bells sounded.

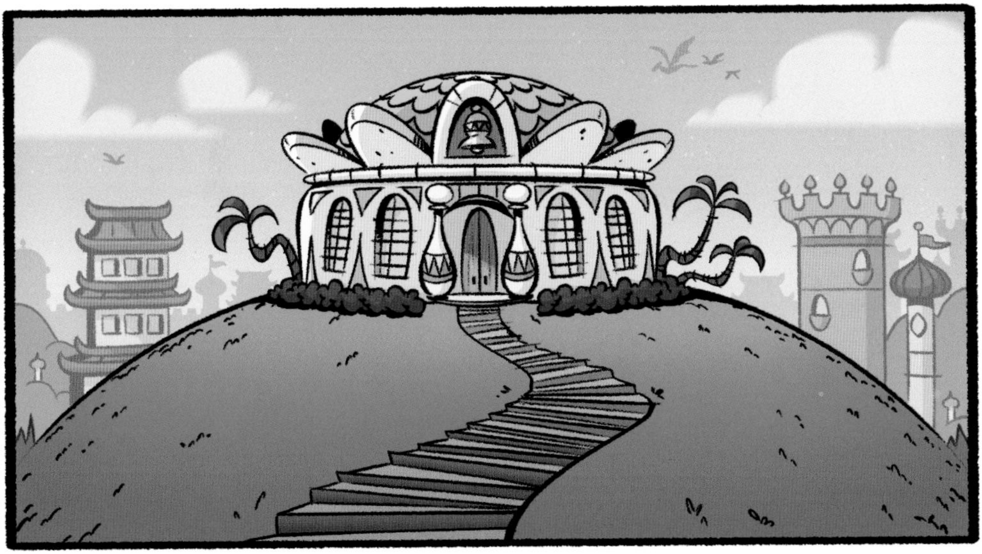

The Spark Day Ceremony was about to begin!

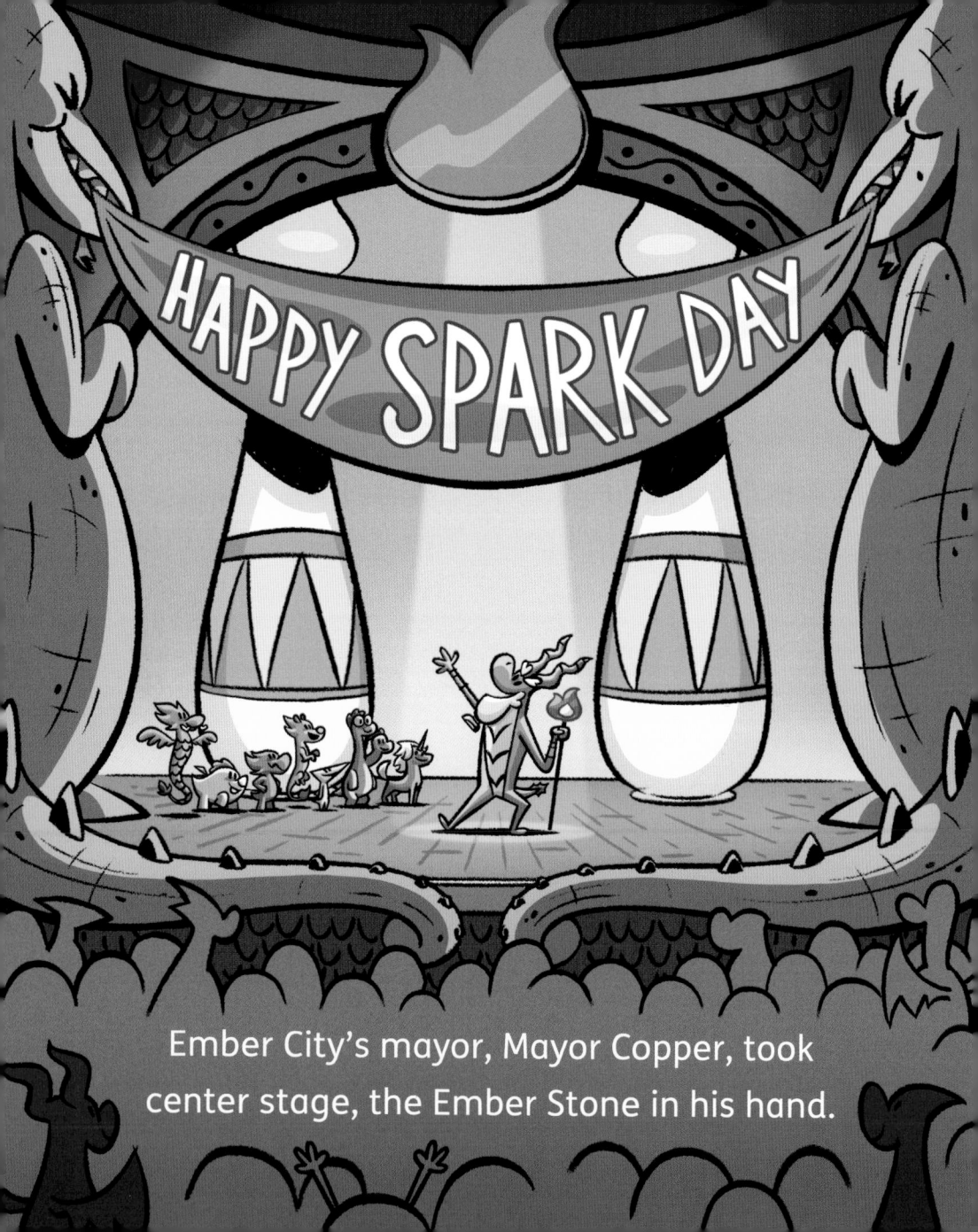

Ember City's mayor, Mayor Copper, took center stage, the Ember Stone in his hand.

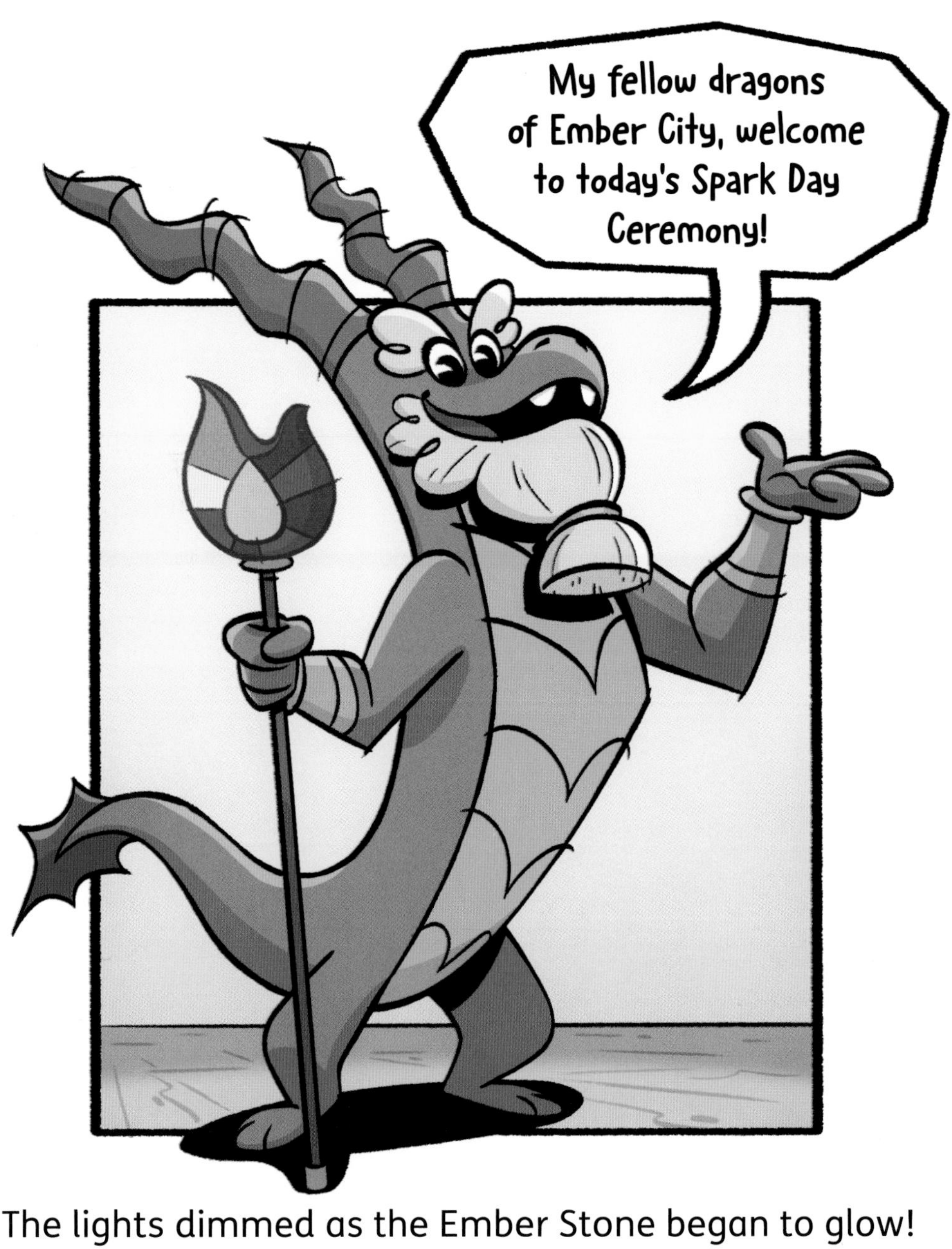
My fellow dragons of Ember City, welcome to today's Spark Day Ceremony!

The lights dimmed as the Ember Stone began to glow!

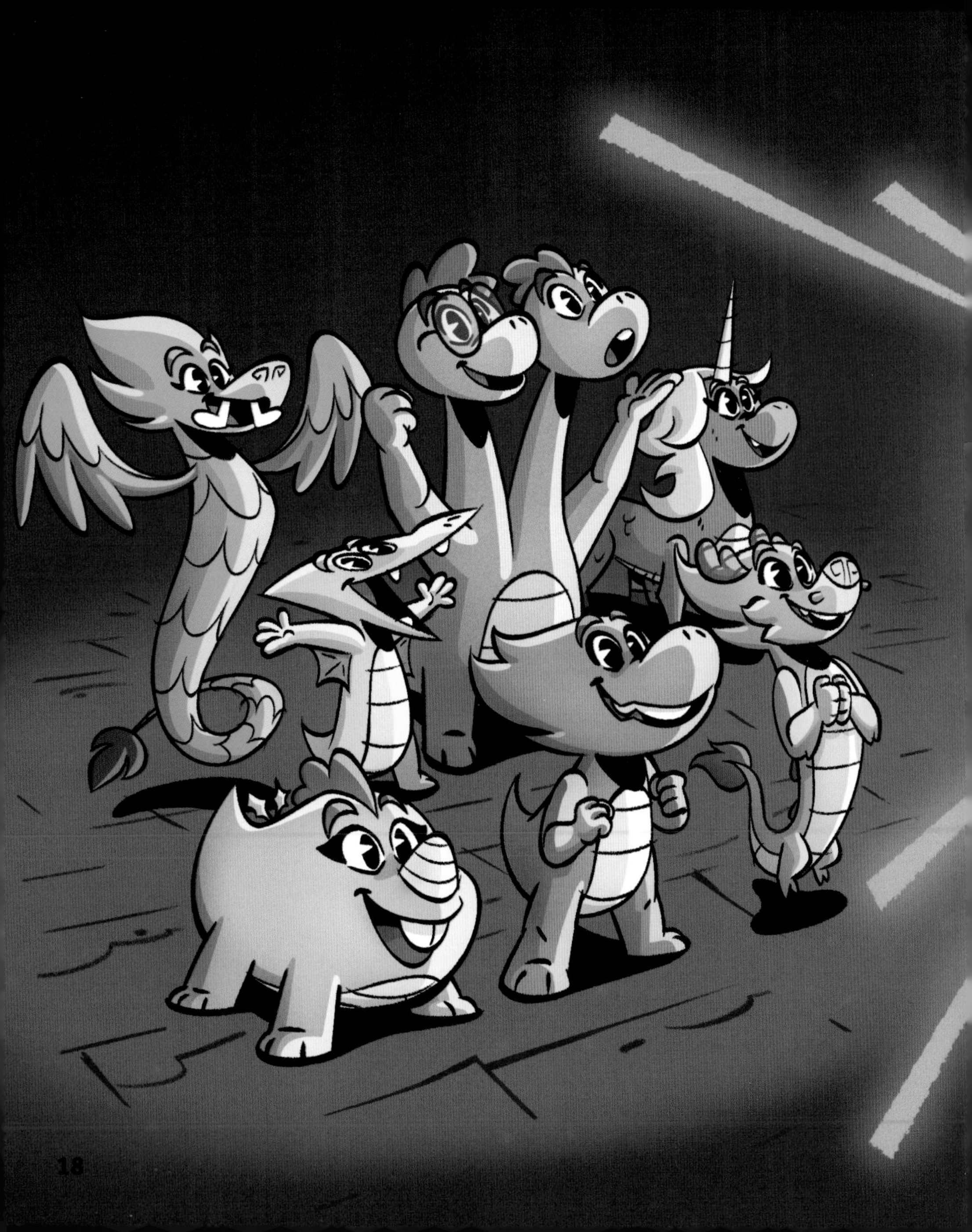

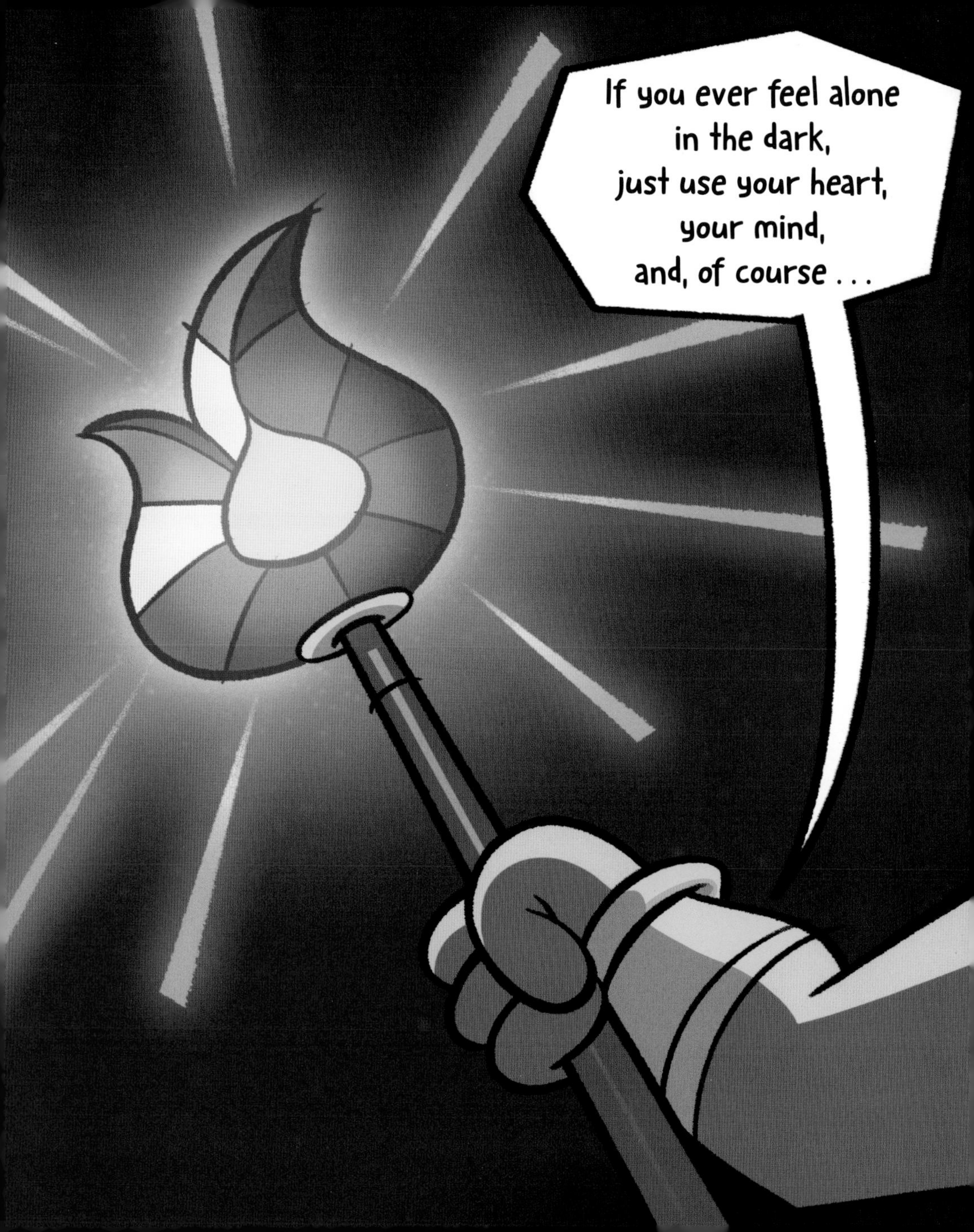
If you ever feel alone
in the dark,
just use your heart,
your mind,
and, of course . . .

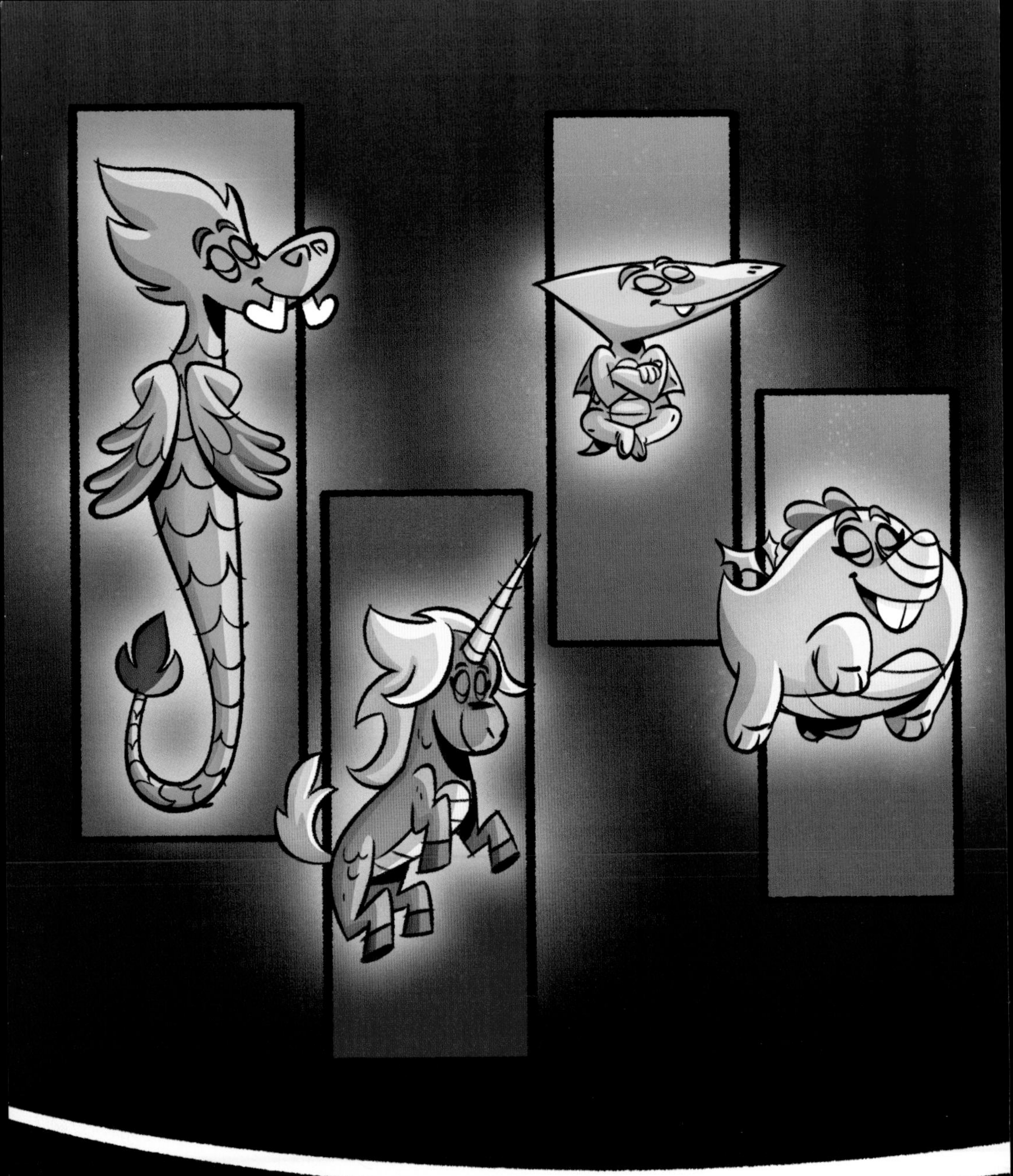

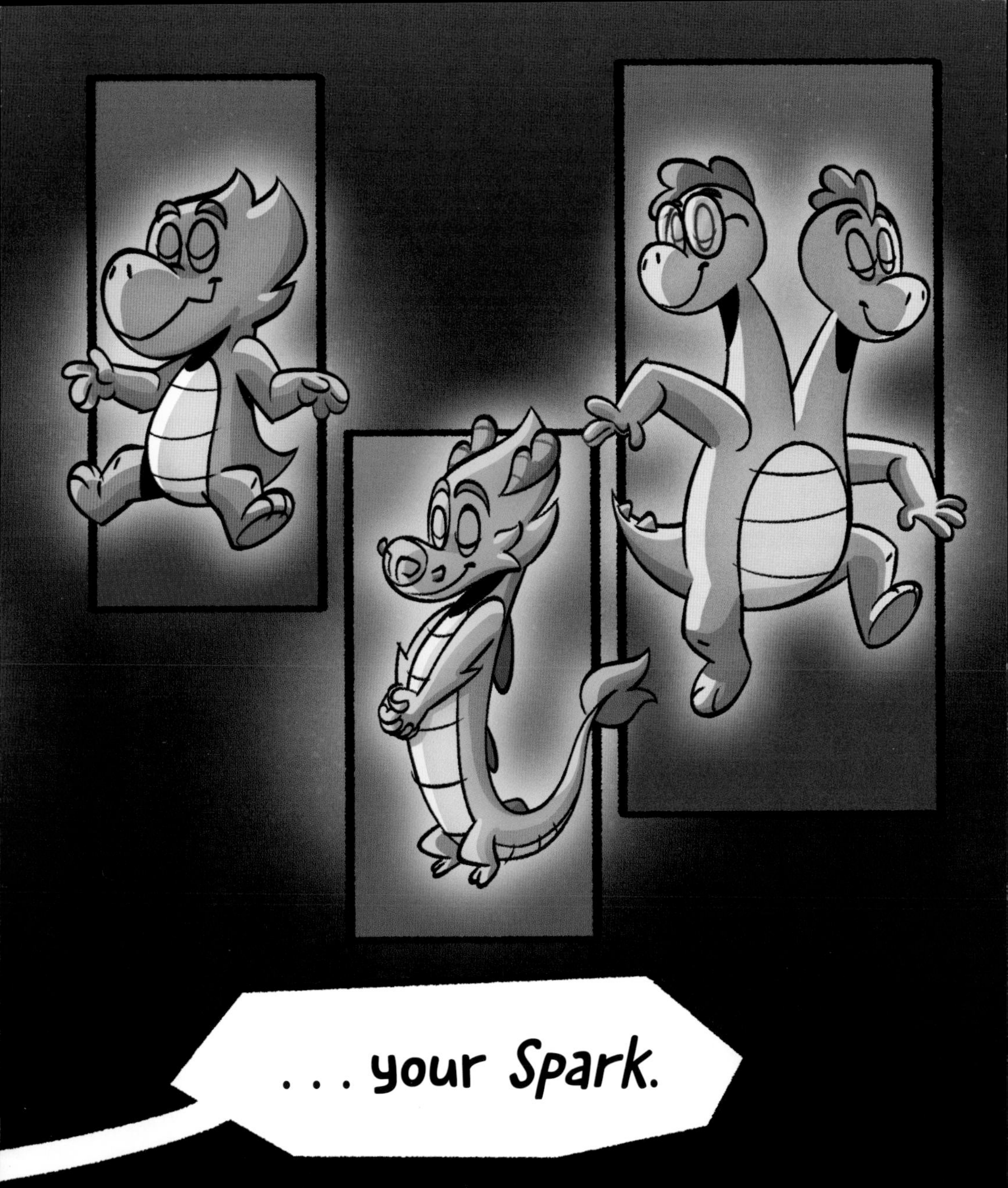
. . . your Spark.

CHAPTER TWO

The glow from the Ember Stone
was seen all throughout Ember City!

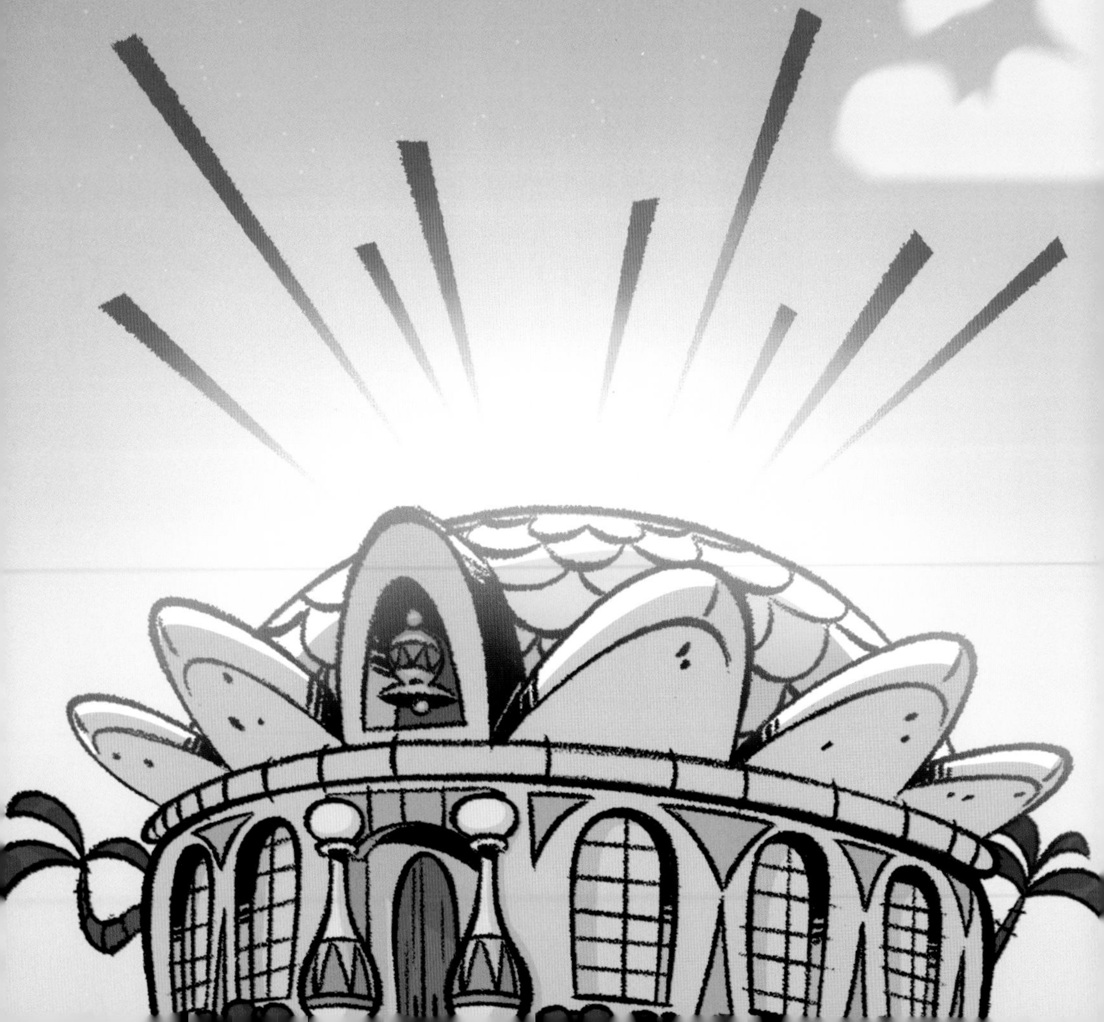

The mayor smiled at the little dragons.

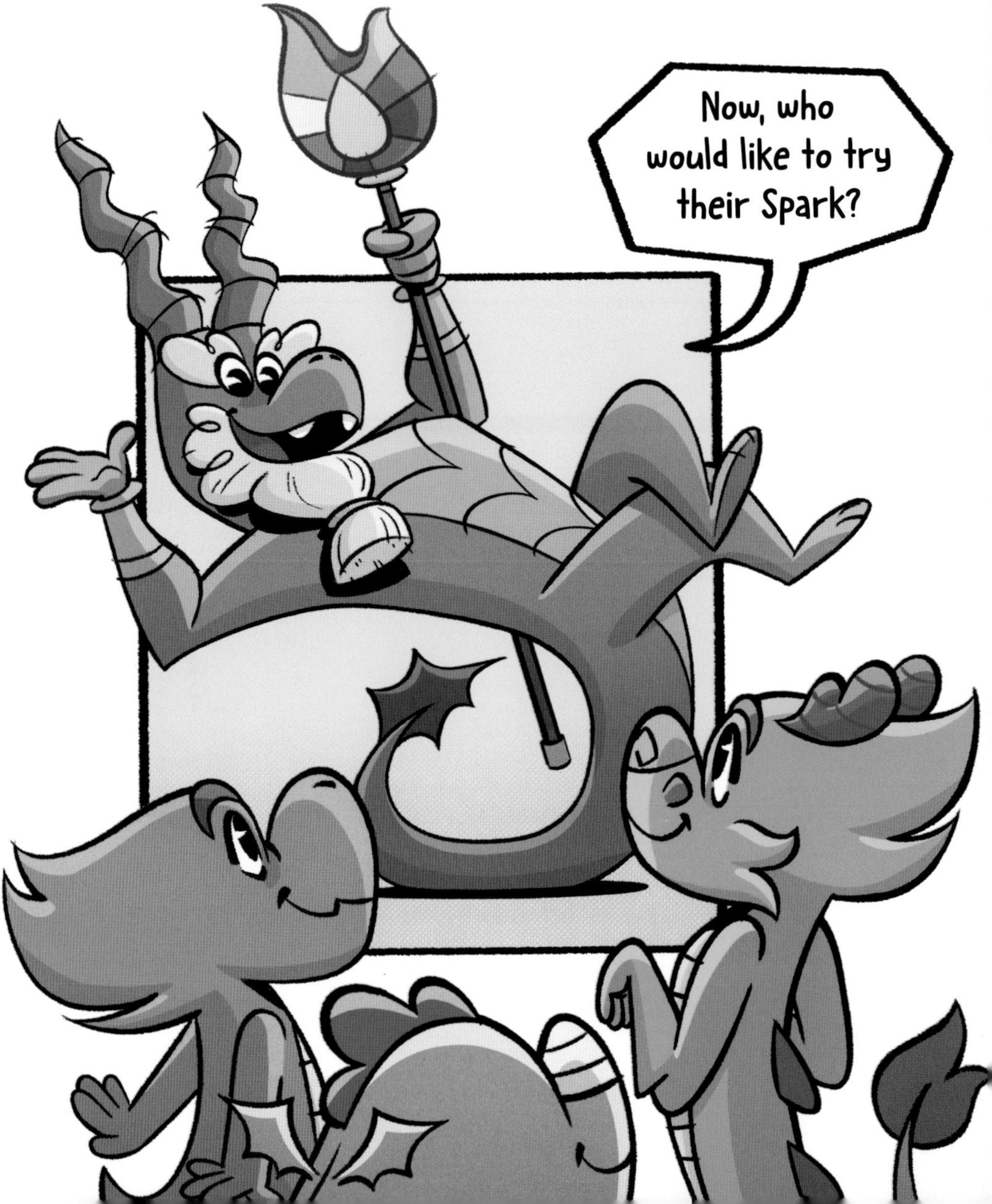
Now, who would like to try their Spark?

At first everyone was silent.
But then Runa stepped forward.

She shivered and let out her
magical breath.

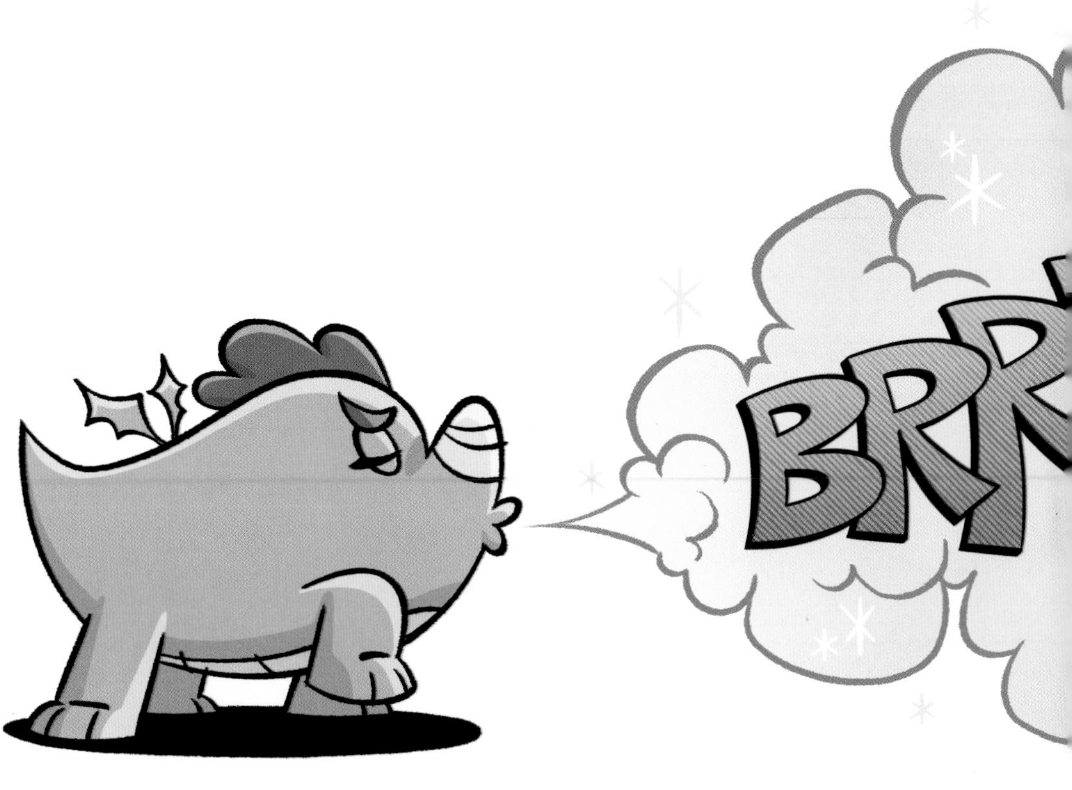
BRR

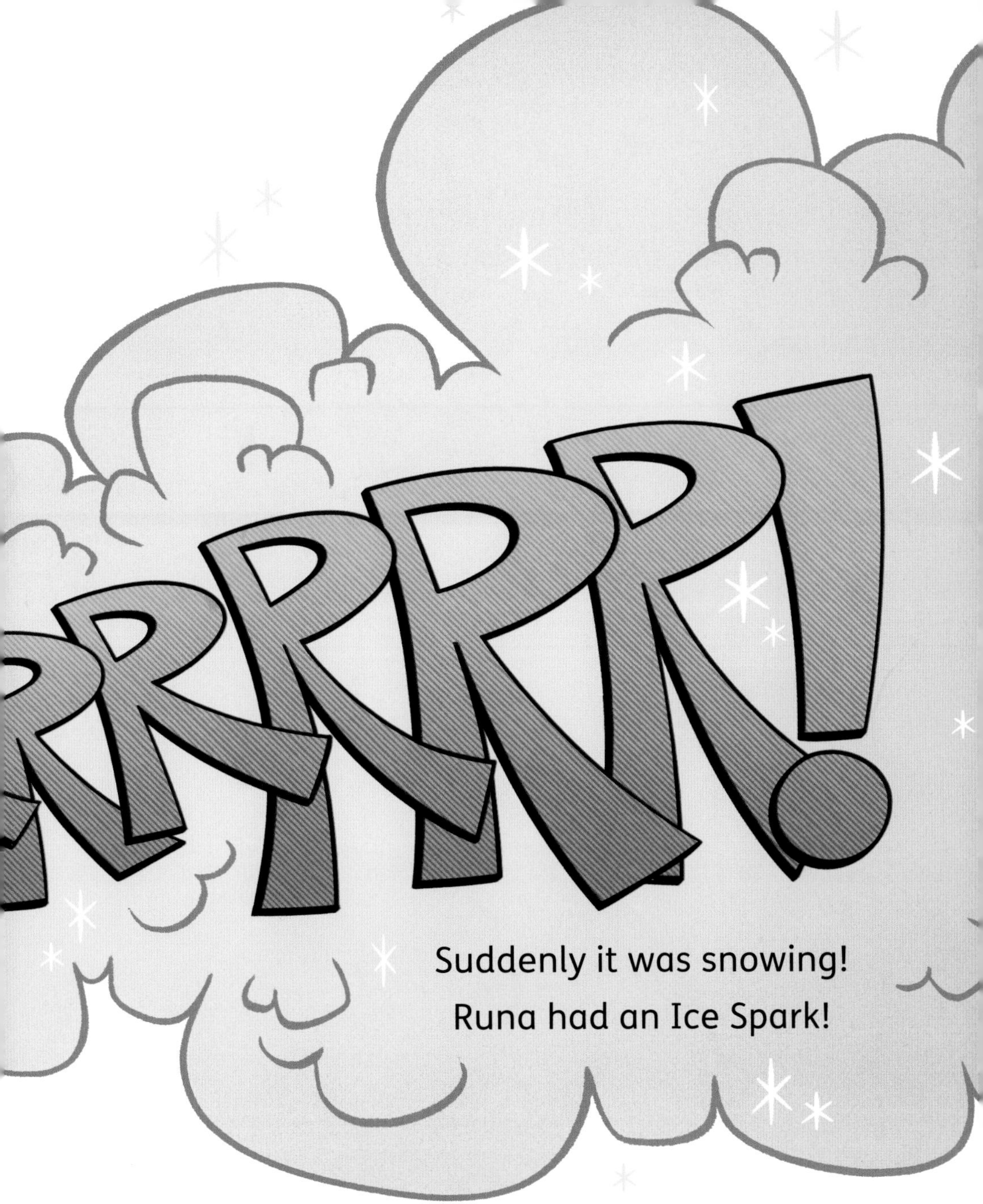
RRRR!

Suddenly it was snowing!

Runa had an Ice Spark!

Next it was Li's turn.

He felt a tickle in his nose and sneezed!

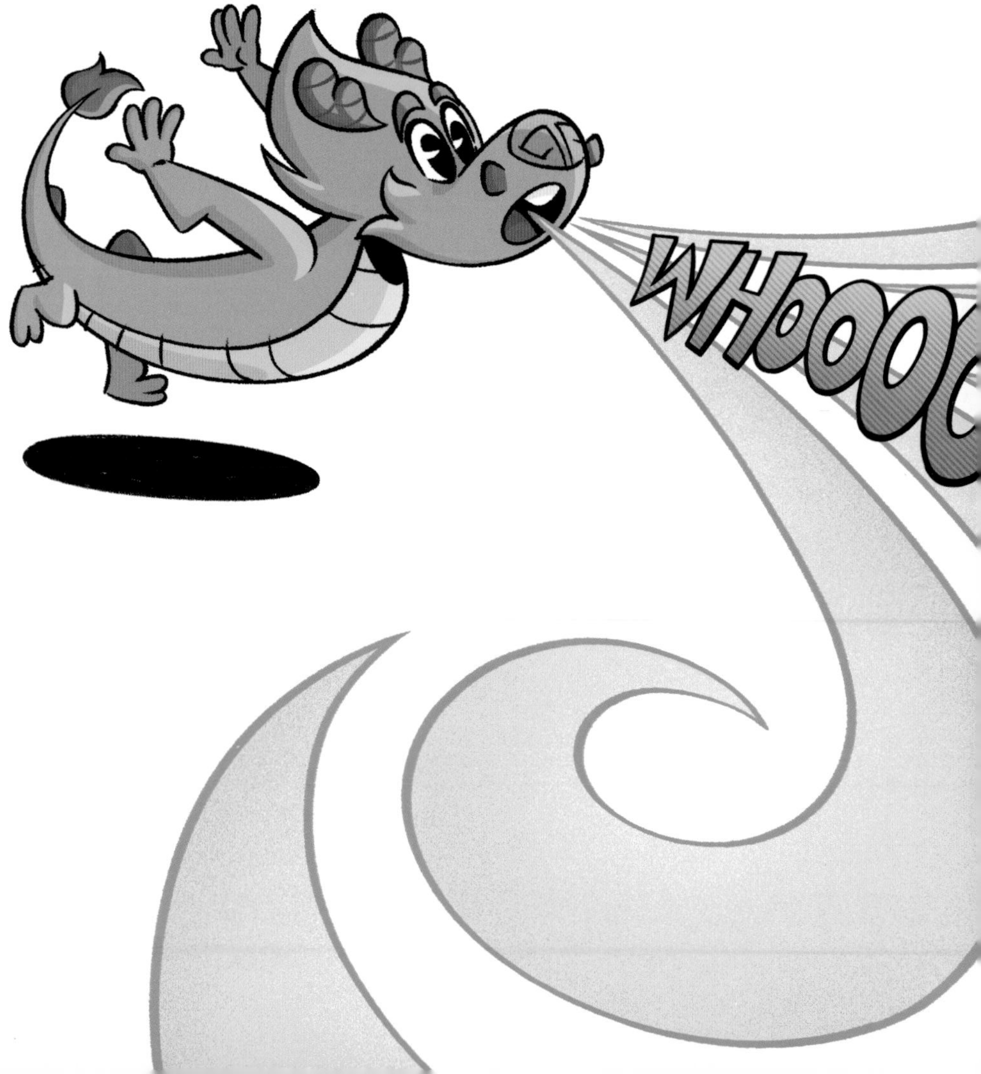
WHOOO

A gust of air swirled around the room!

Li had a Wind Spark!

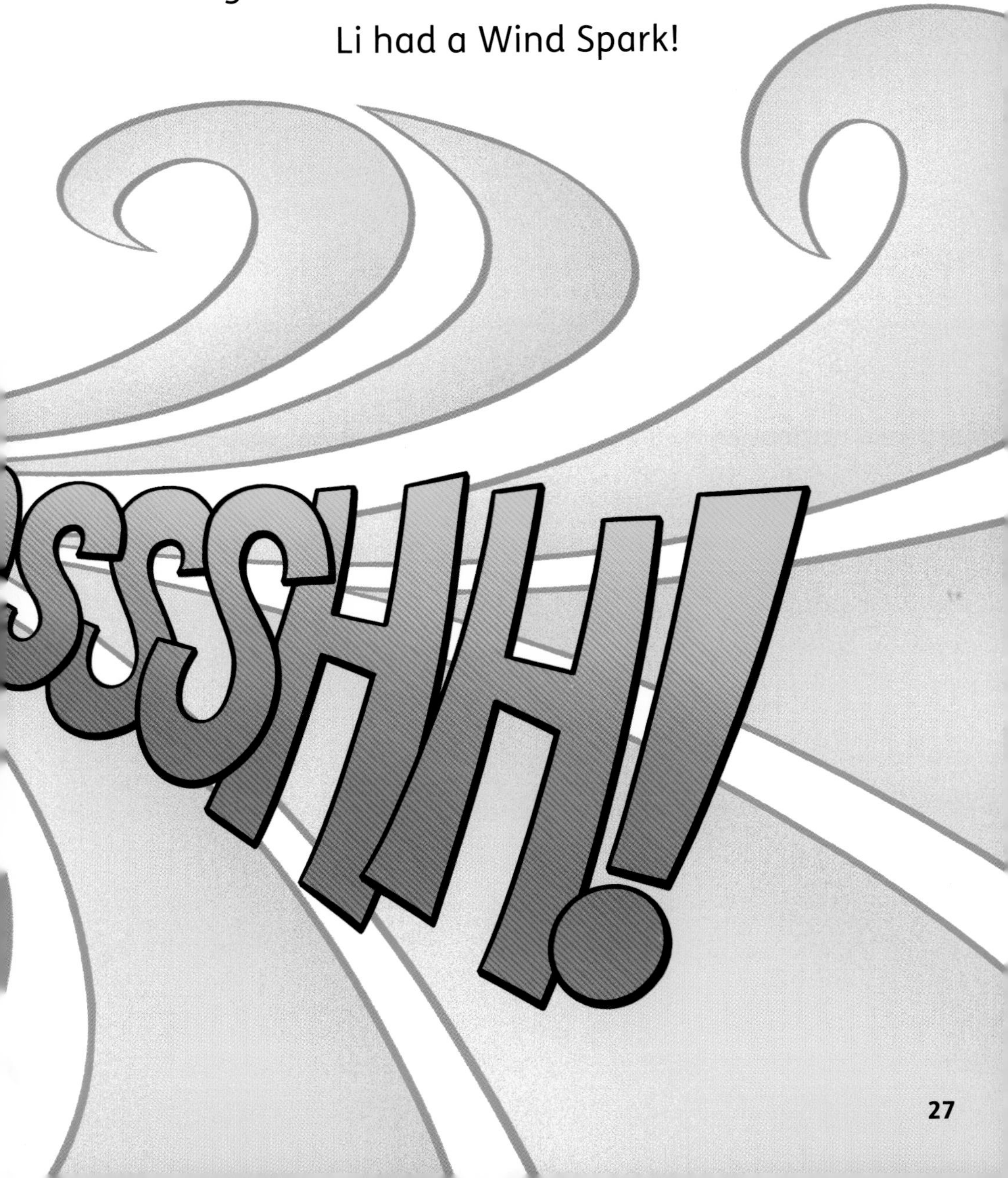
SSSHH!

Drake jumped forward for his turn.
He knew his Spark was going to be big.
He could *feel* it!

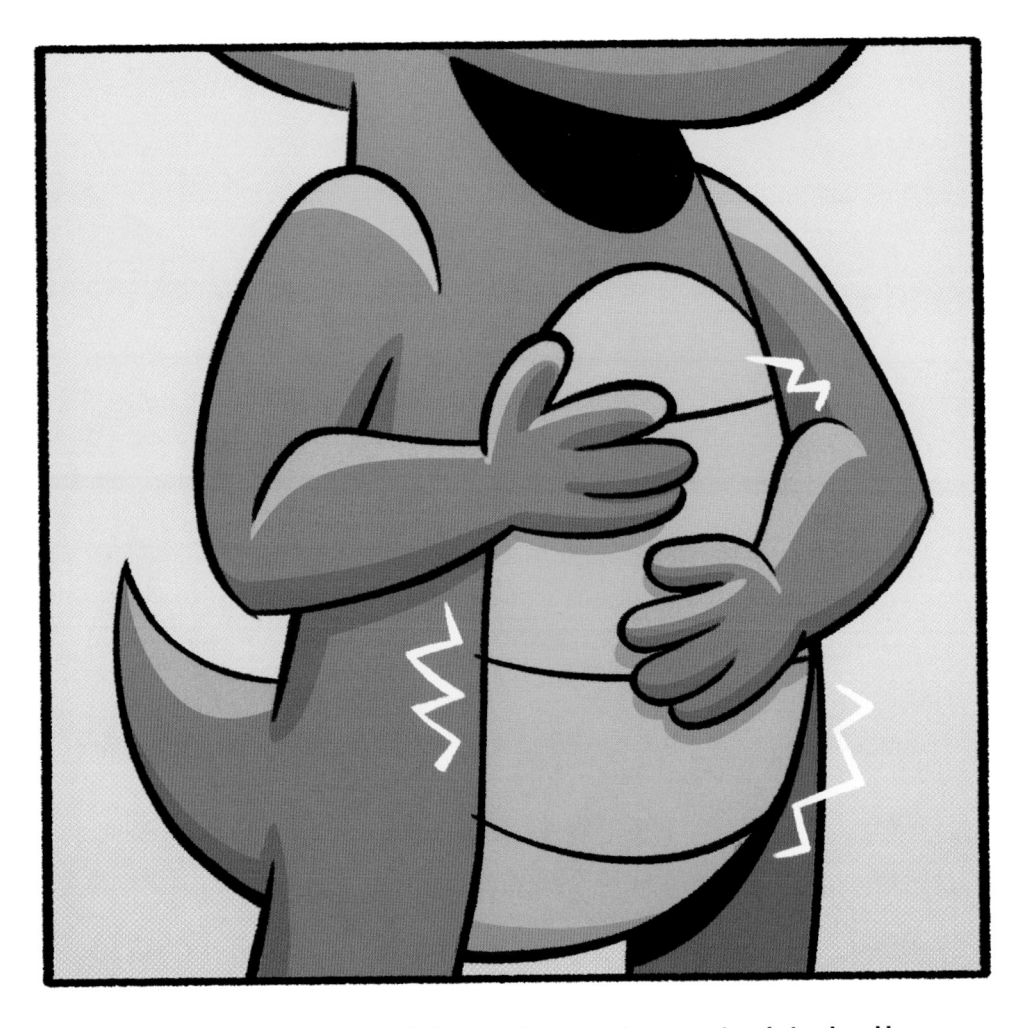

Drake felt a rumbling deep down in his belly.

And with a giant roar . . .

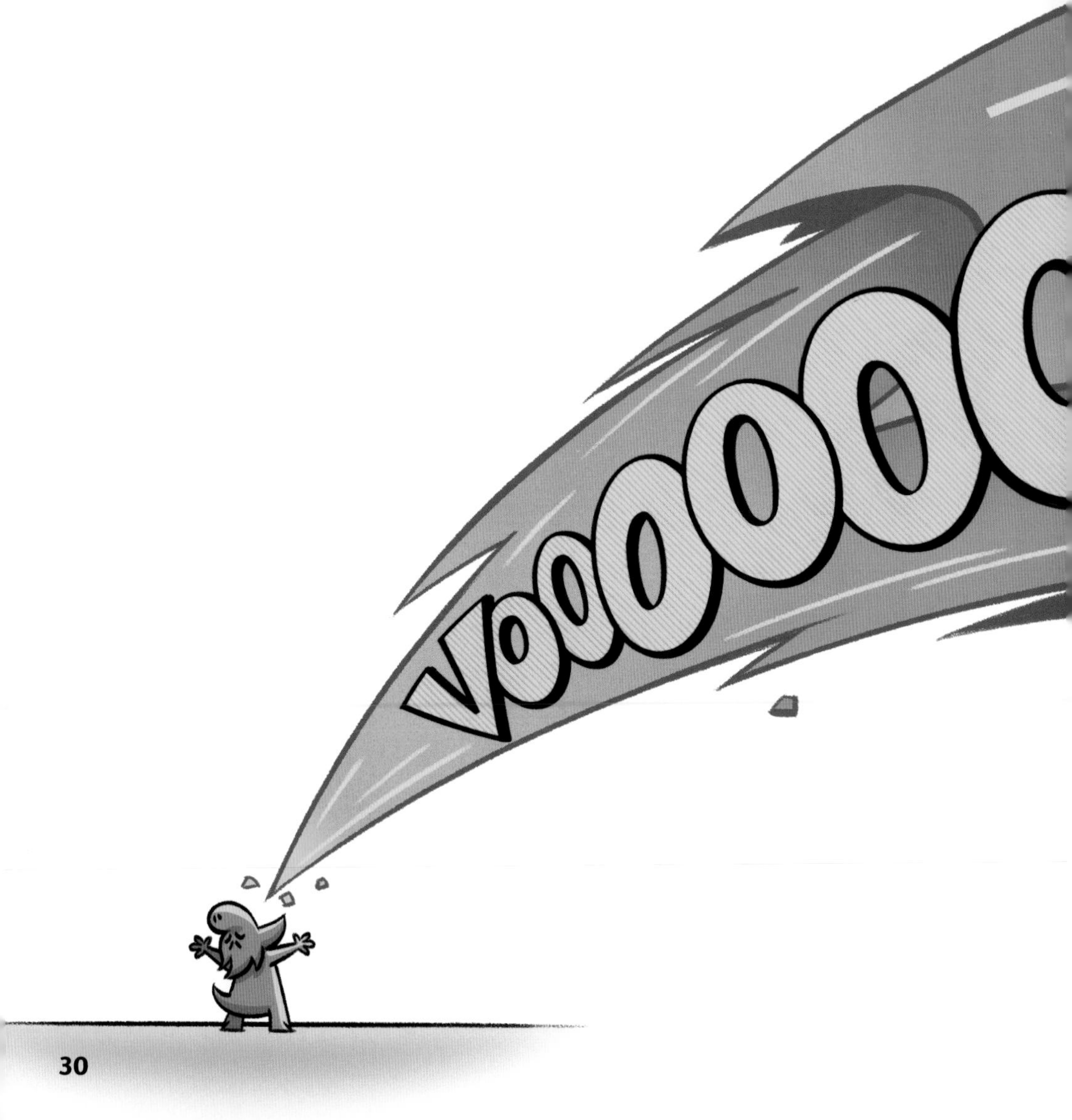
VOOOOOOO

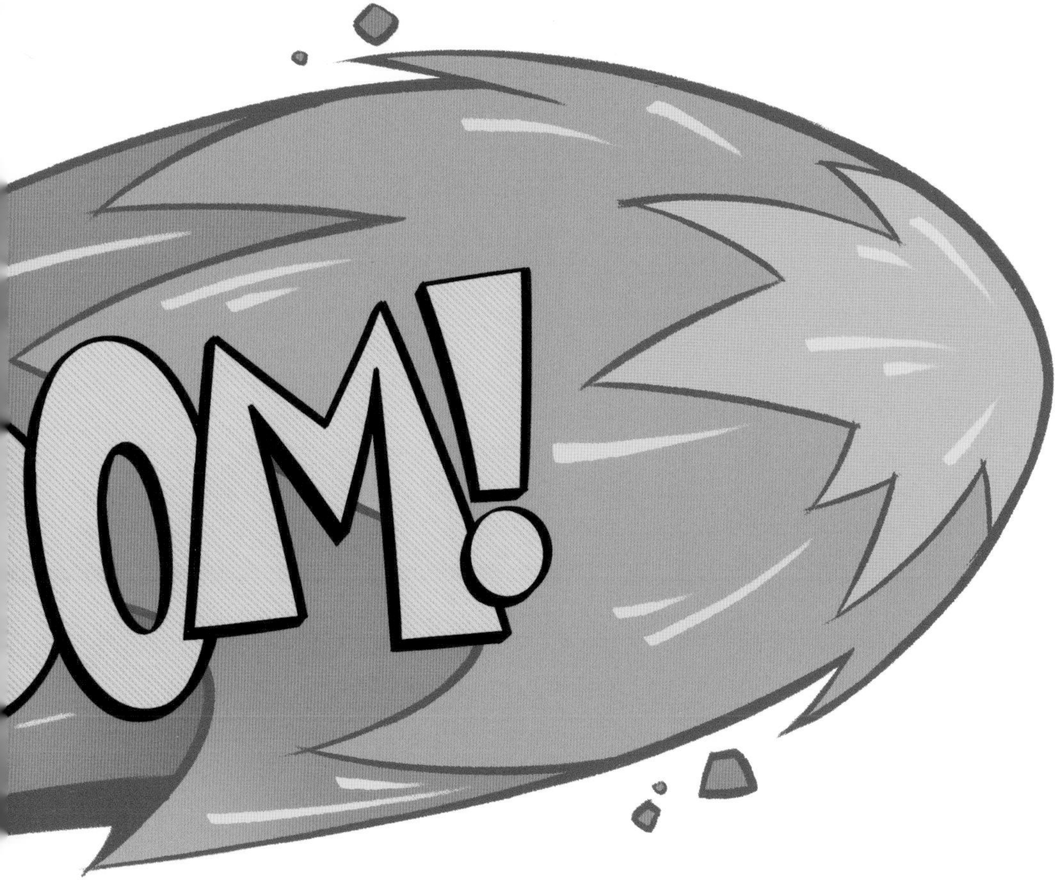
OM!

Drake released a burst of his Energy Spark!

Fizz went next.

His tummy glowed with light before
his Spark bolted outward!

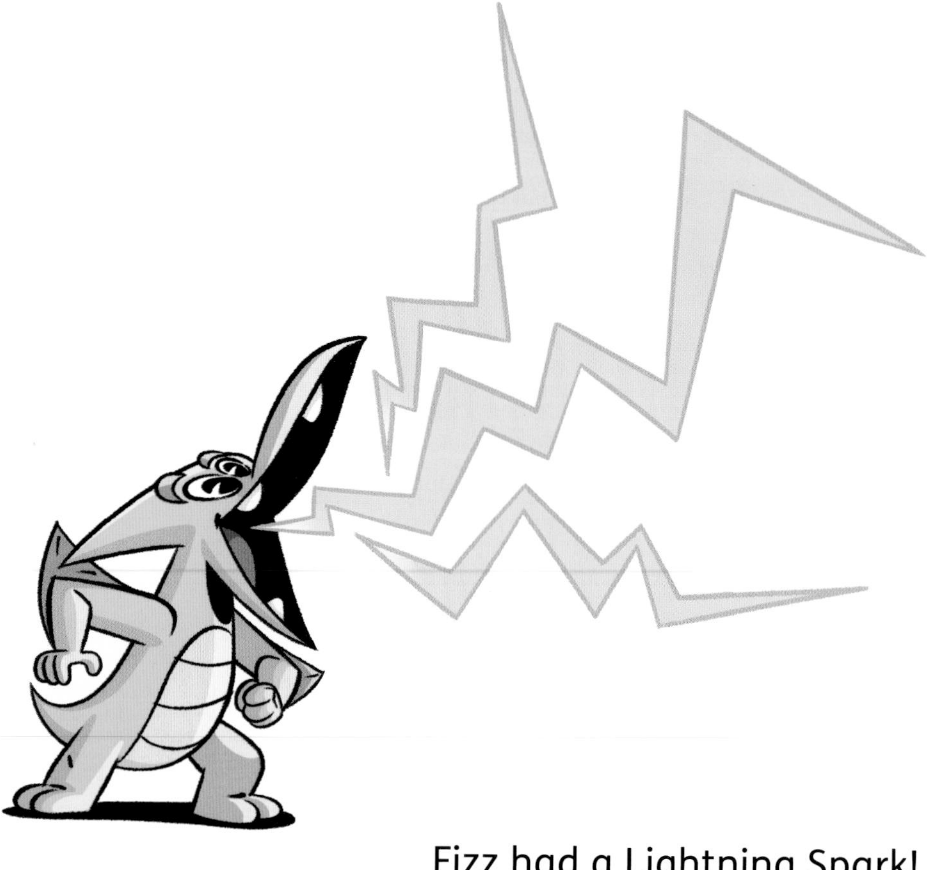

Fizz had a Lightning Spark!

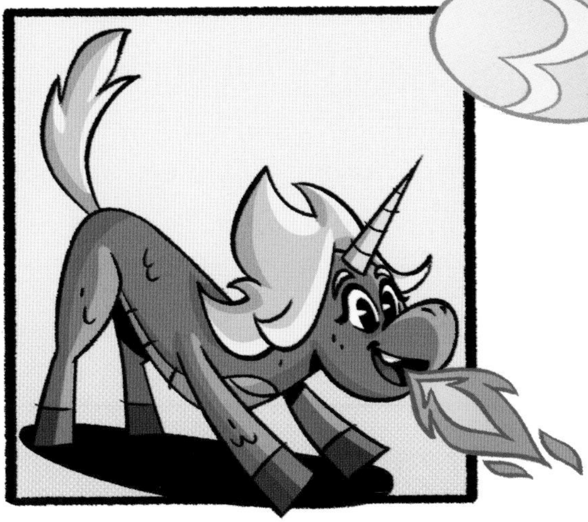

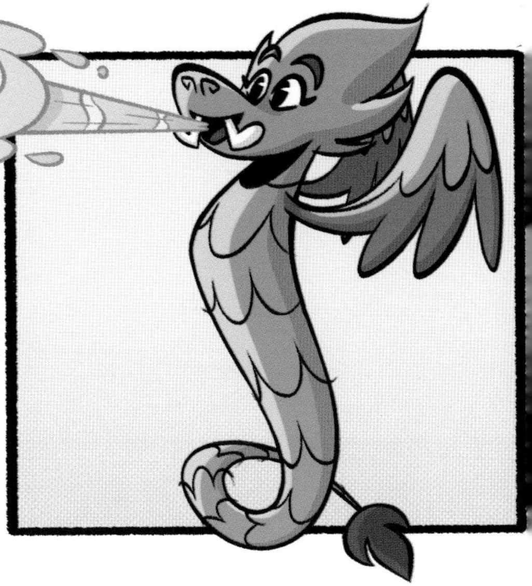

One by one the rest of the young dragons showed off their new Sparks.

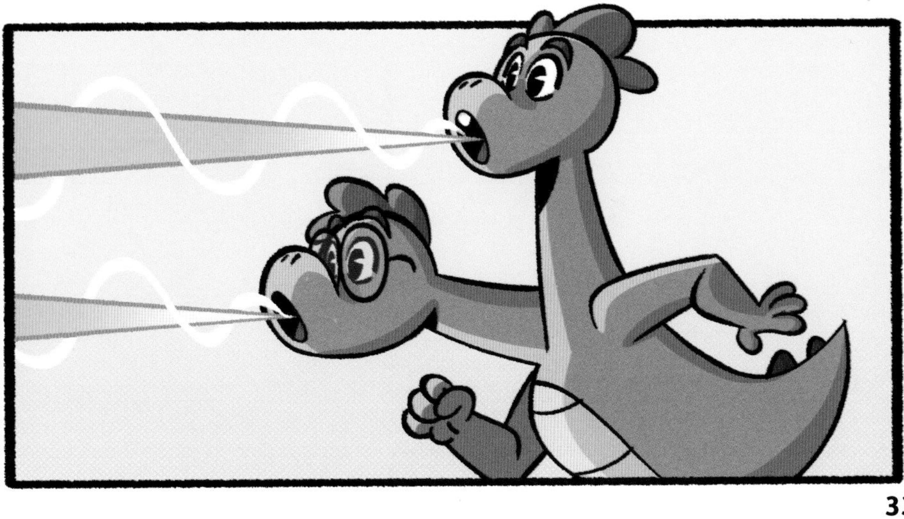

When the ceremony was over, Mayor Copper had a few parting words for the little dragons.

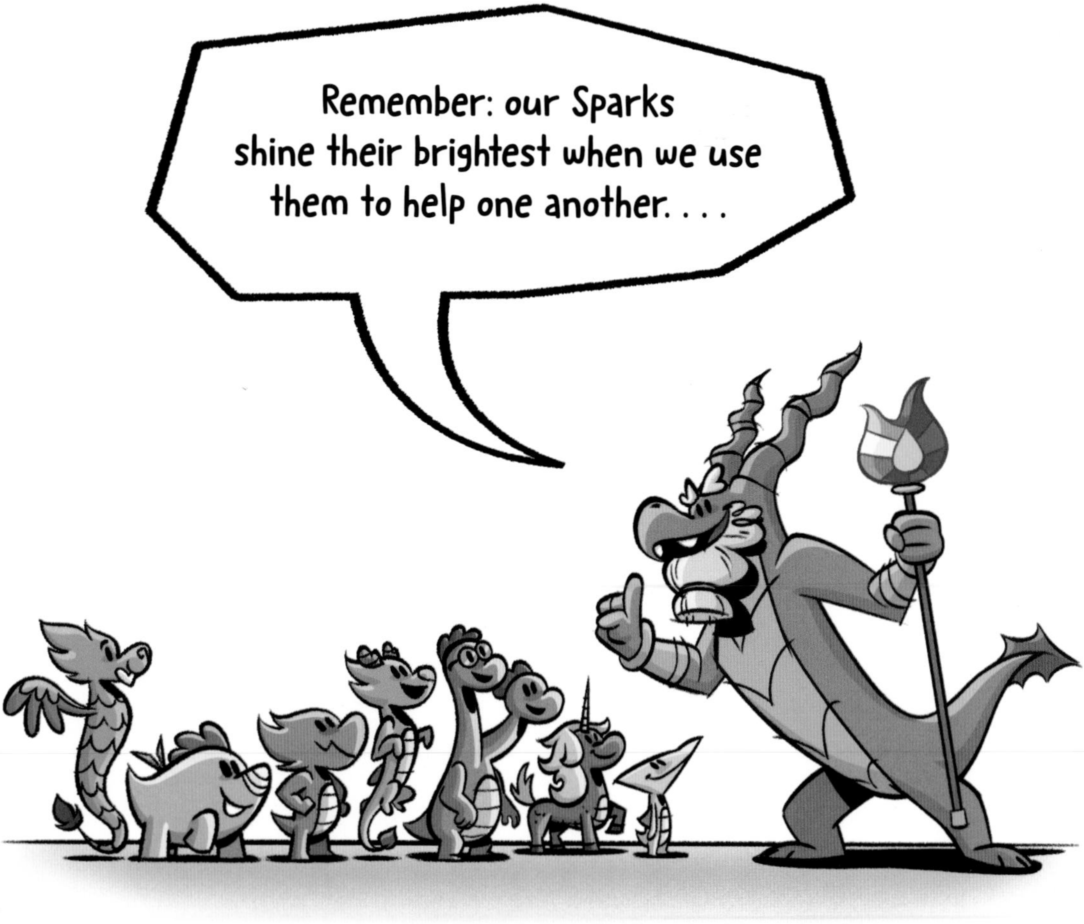
Remember: our Sparks shine their brightest when we use them to help one another. . . .

CHAPTER THREE

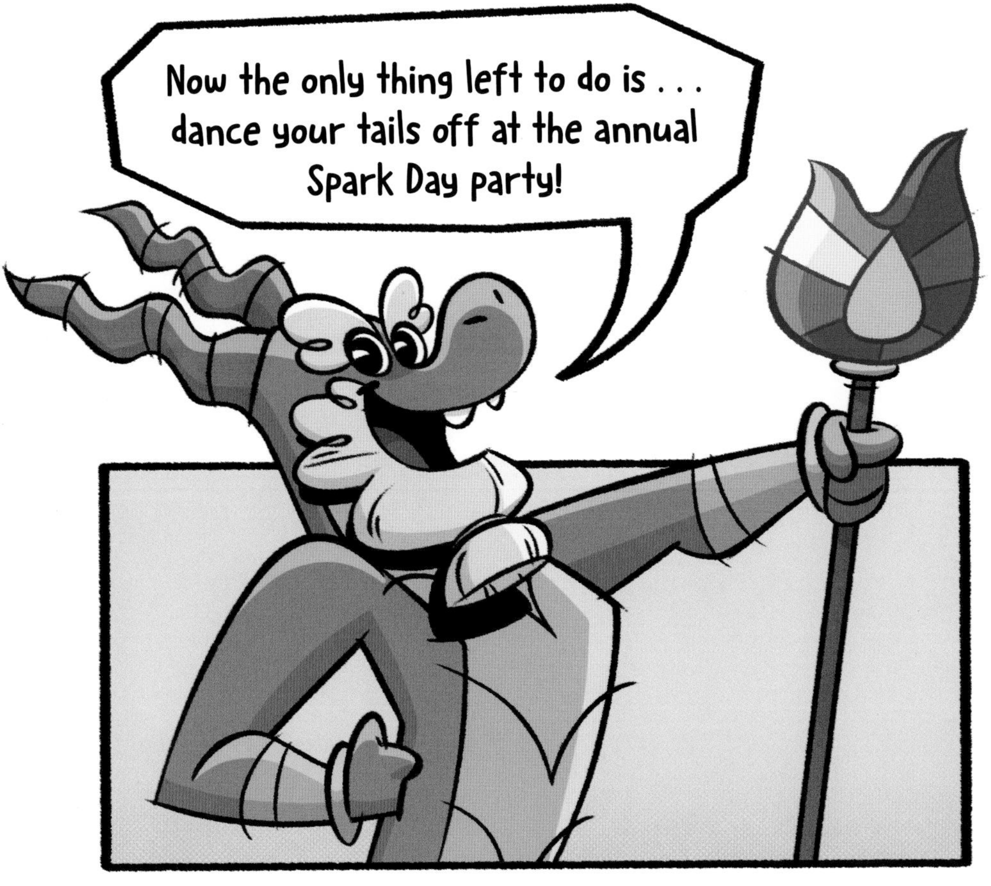
Now the only thing left to do is . . . dance your tails off at the annual Spark Day party!

It was a day of firsts for the three friends.
They had never been to a Spark Day party before.

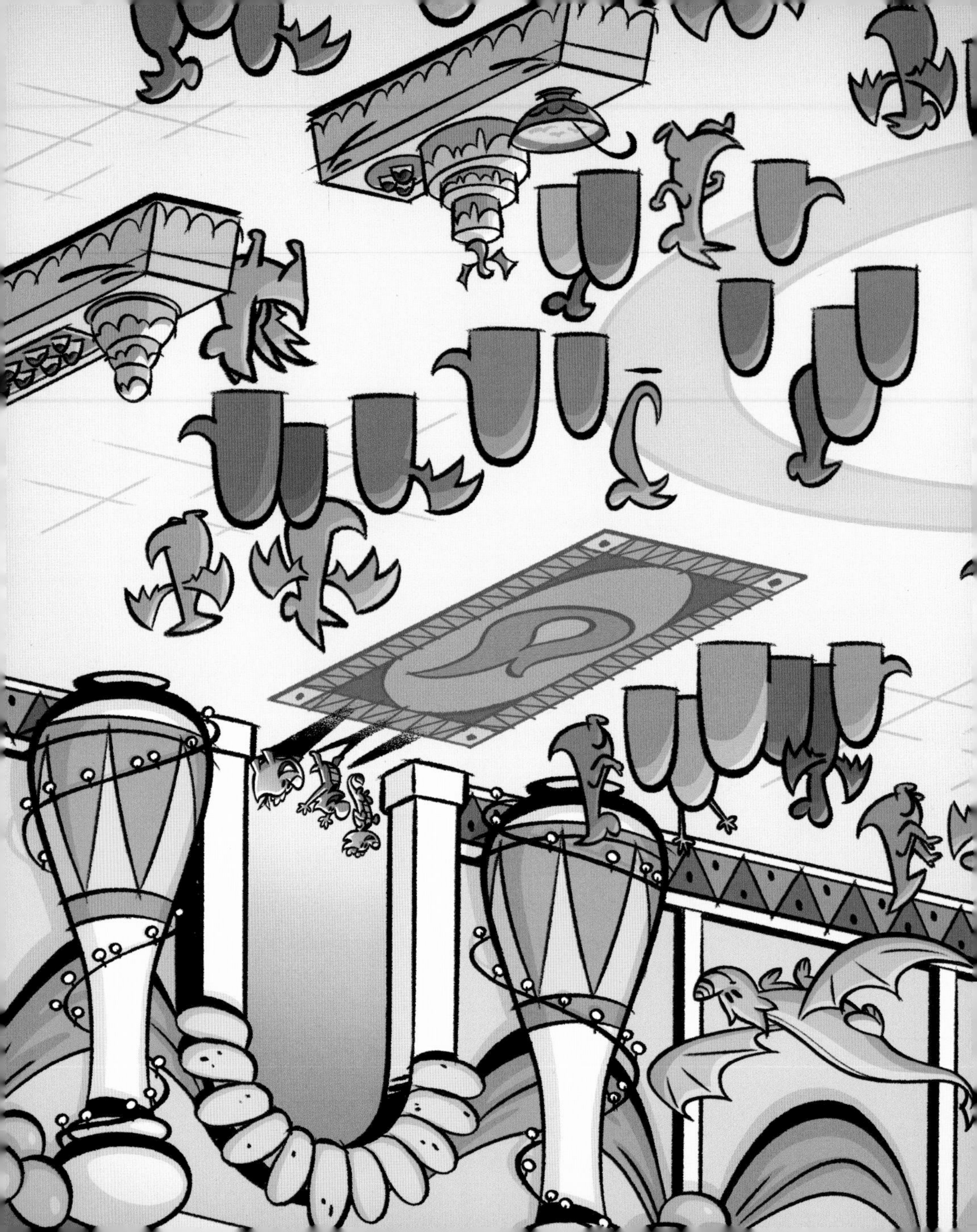

Drake, Li, and Runa didn't think their magical day could get any better.

But then they walked into the party and were amazed all over again.

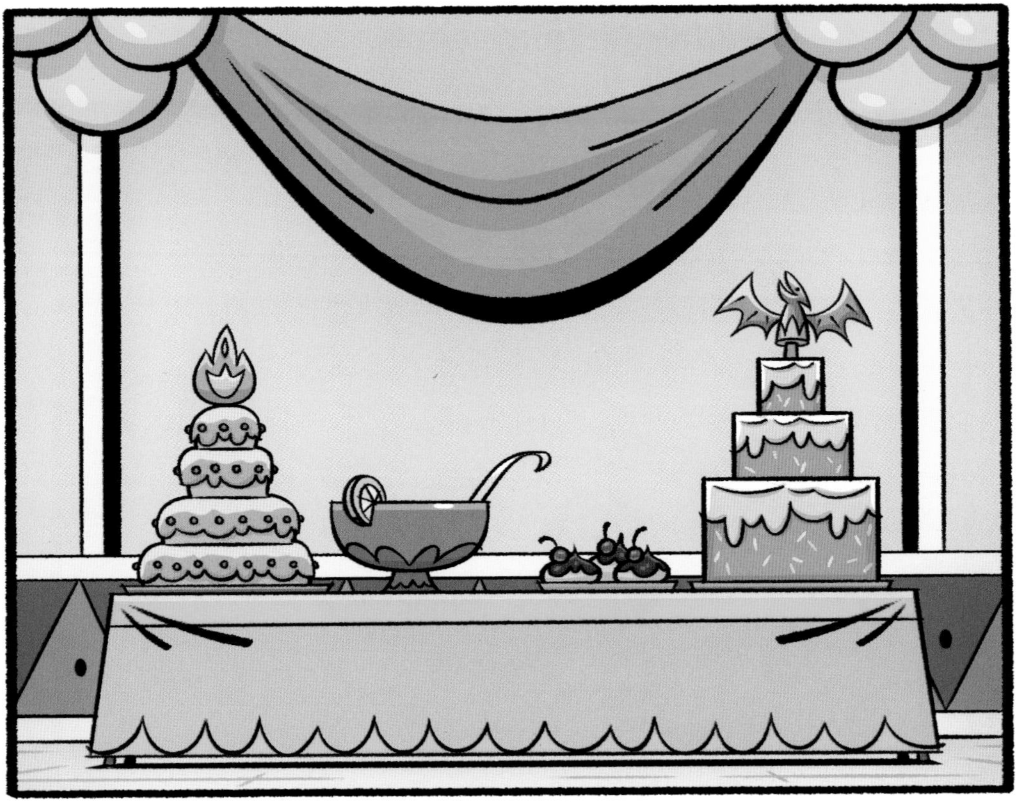

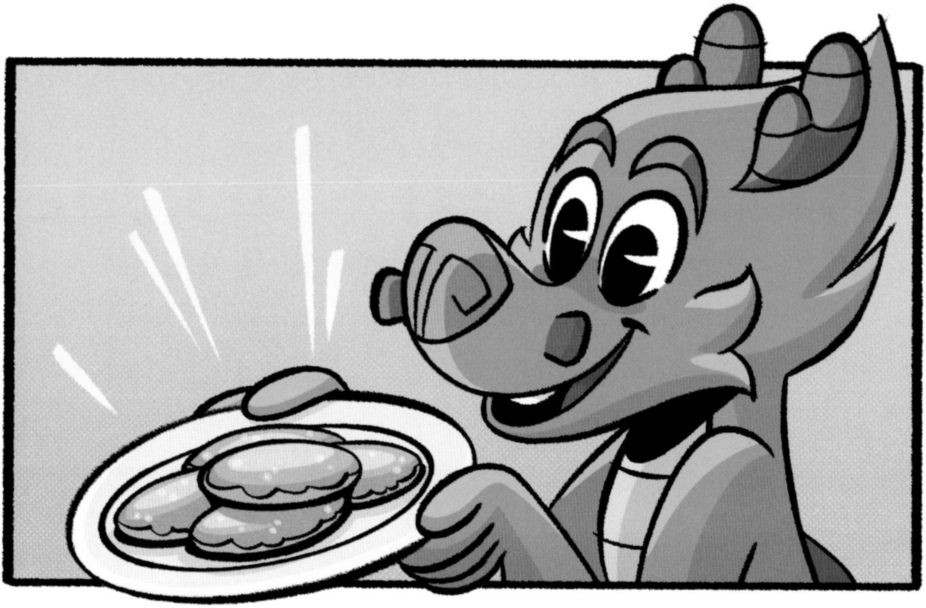

Sugar bite cookies!

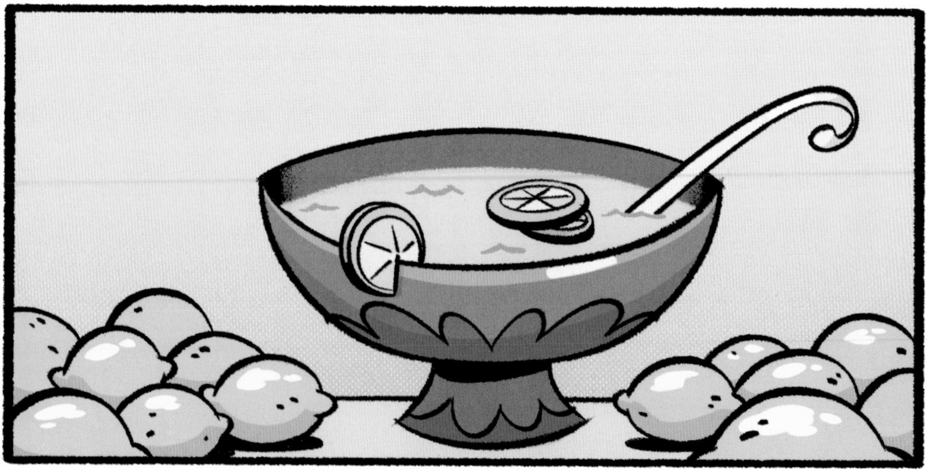

Lemon drop fruit punch!

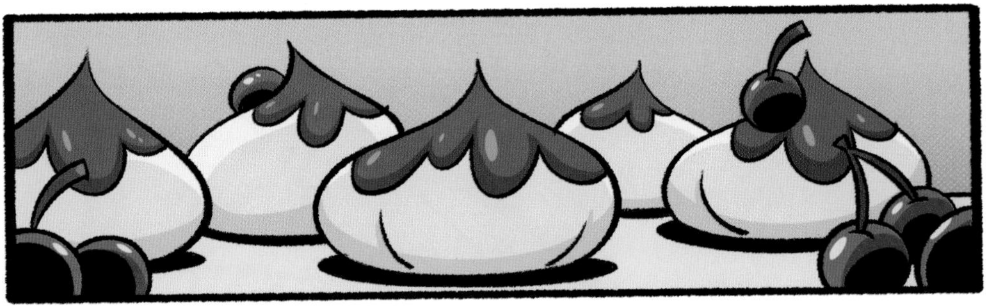

Chocolate cherry dumplings!

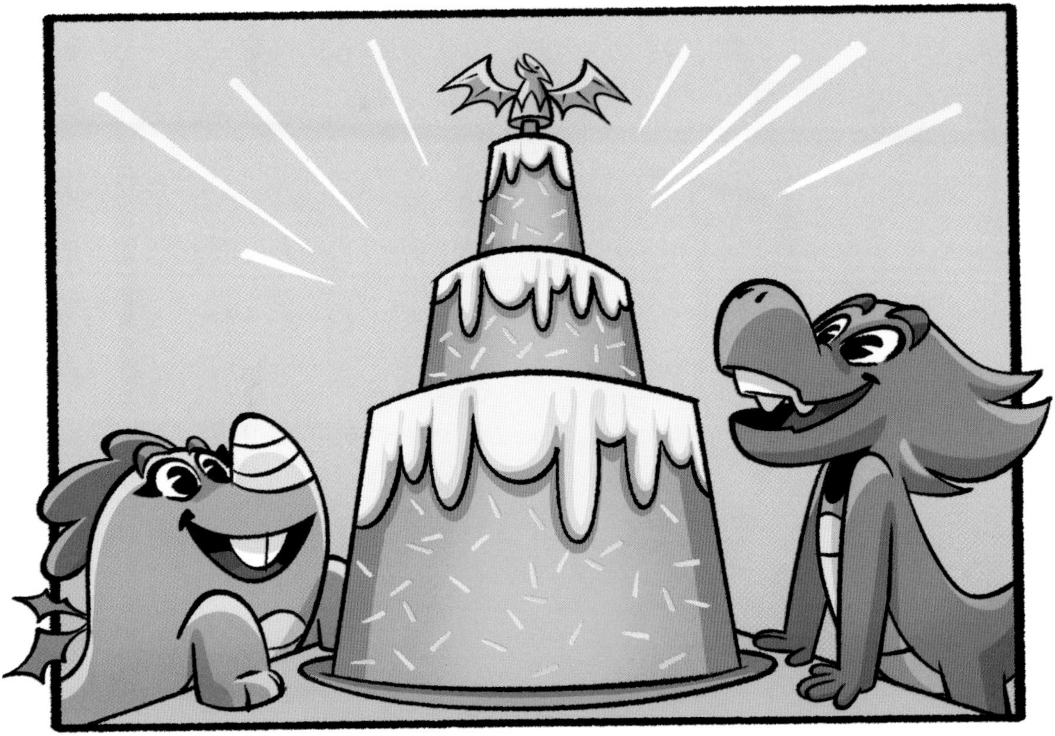

Sparkly sprinkle cake!

And most amazing of all . . .

The legendary
Spark Day
disco ball!

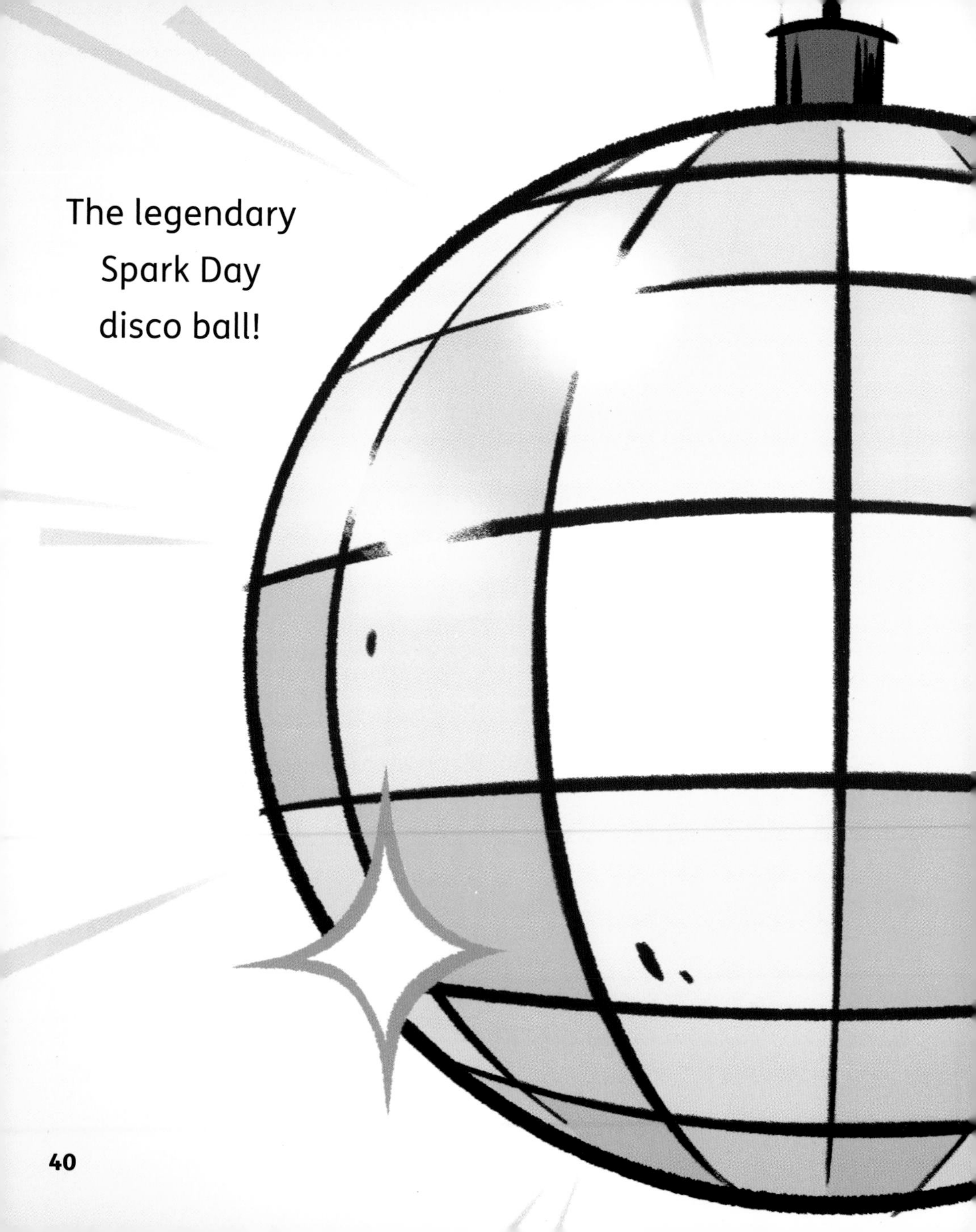

The disco ball was made with the Sparks from all the dragons on the very first Spark Day.

It had a special glow all its own, like the brightest stars in the night sky.

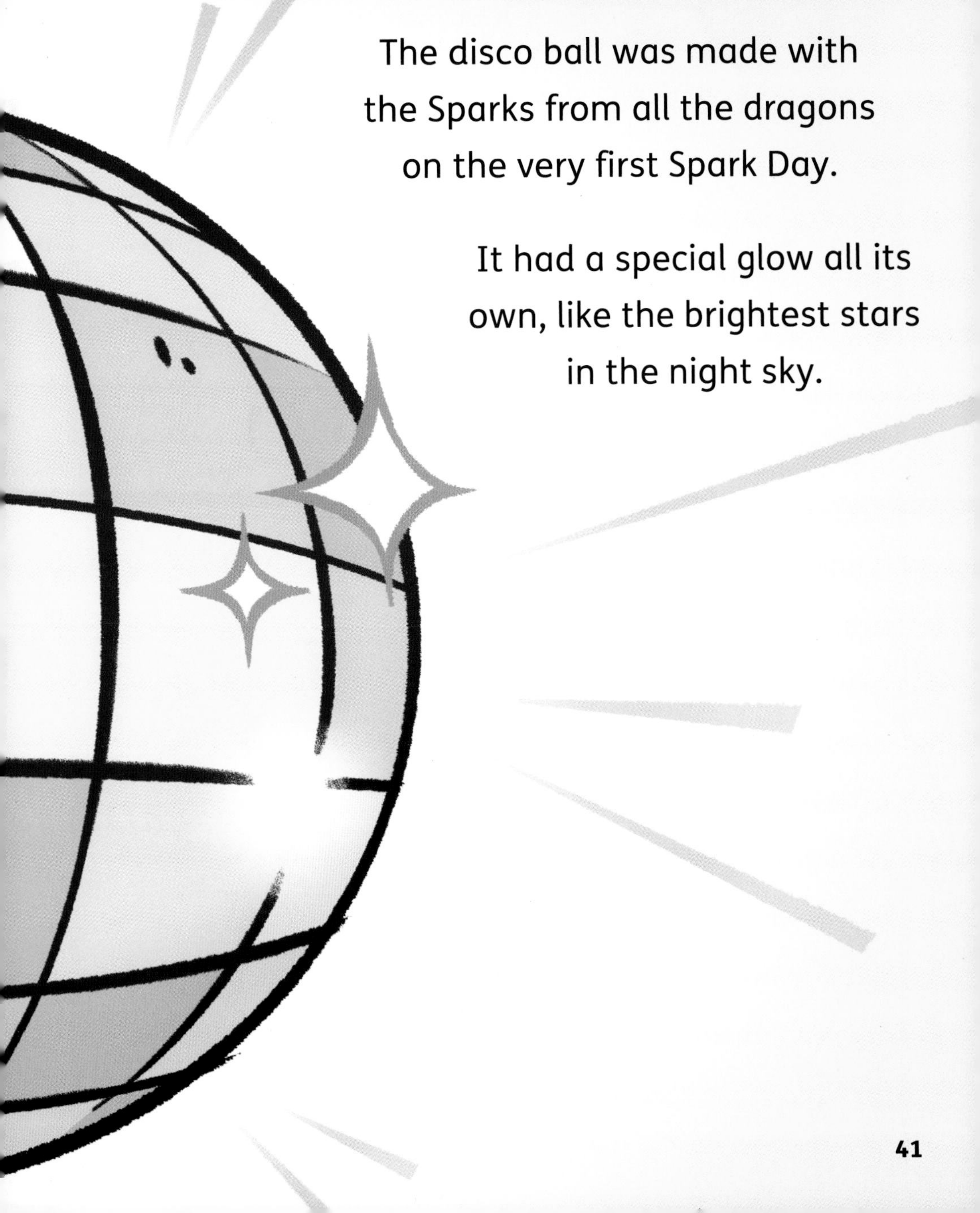

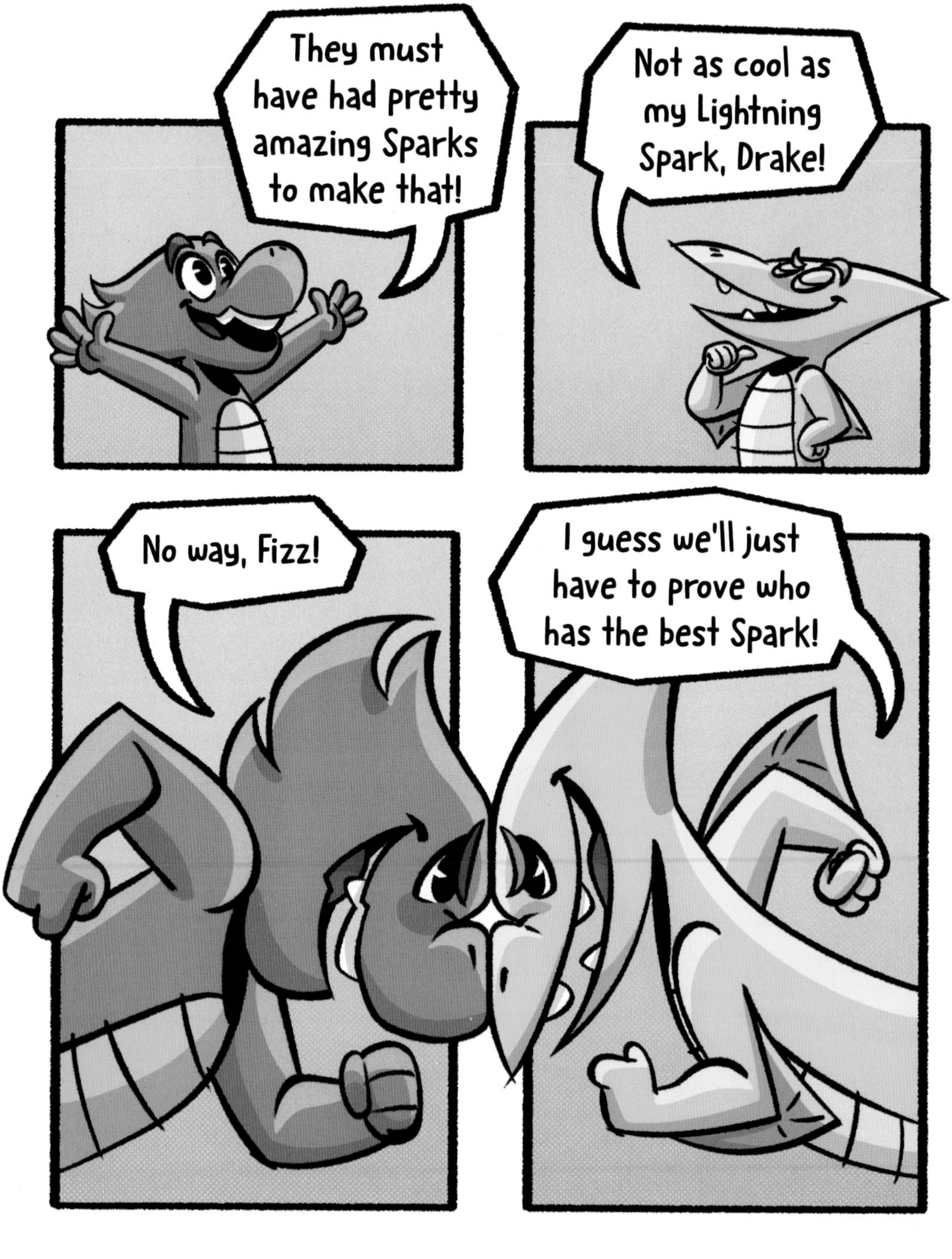
They must have had pretty amazing Sparks to make that!
Not as cool as my Lightning Spark, Drake!
No way, Fizz!
I guess we'll just have to prove who has the best Spark!

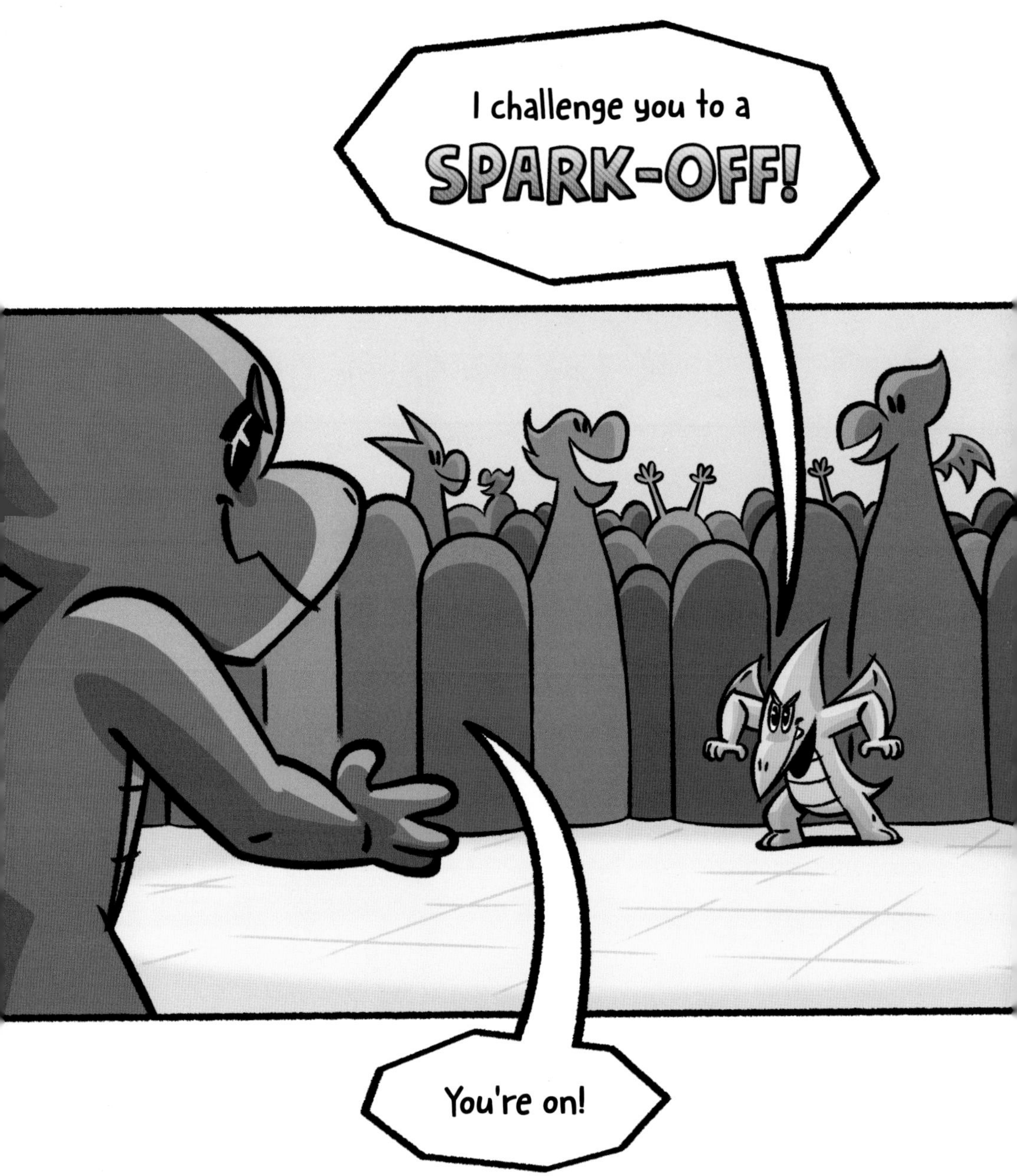
I challenge you to a SPARK-OFF!
You're on!

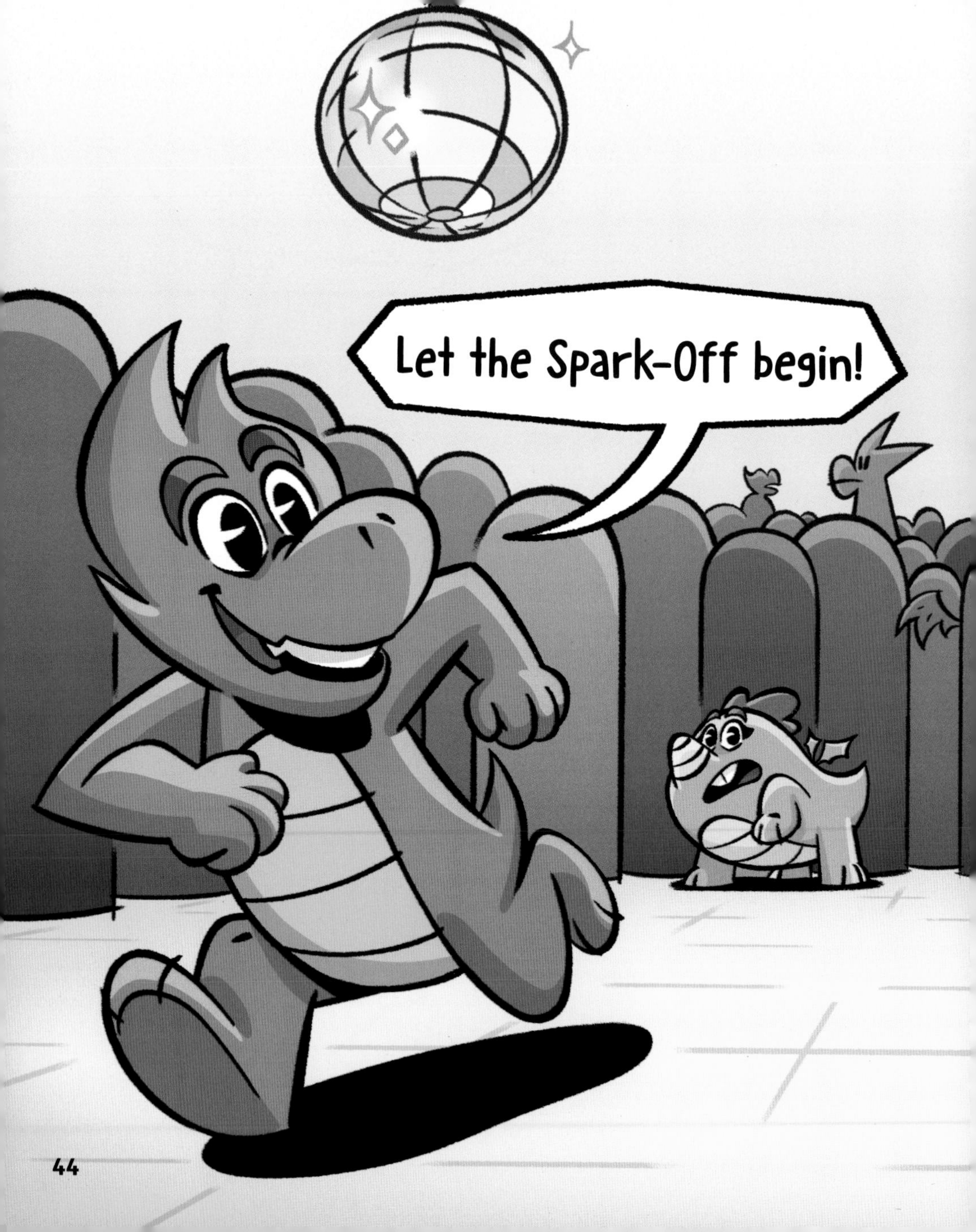
Let the Spark-Off begin!

A hush fell over the crowd as the dance floor cleared for the Spark-Off!

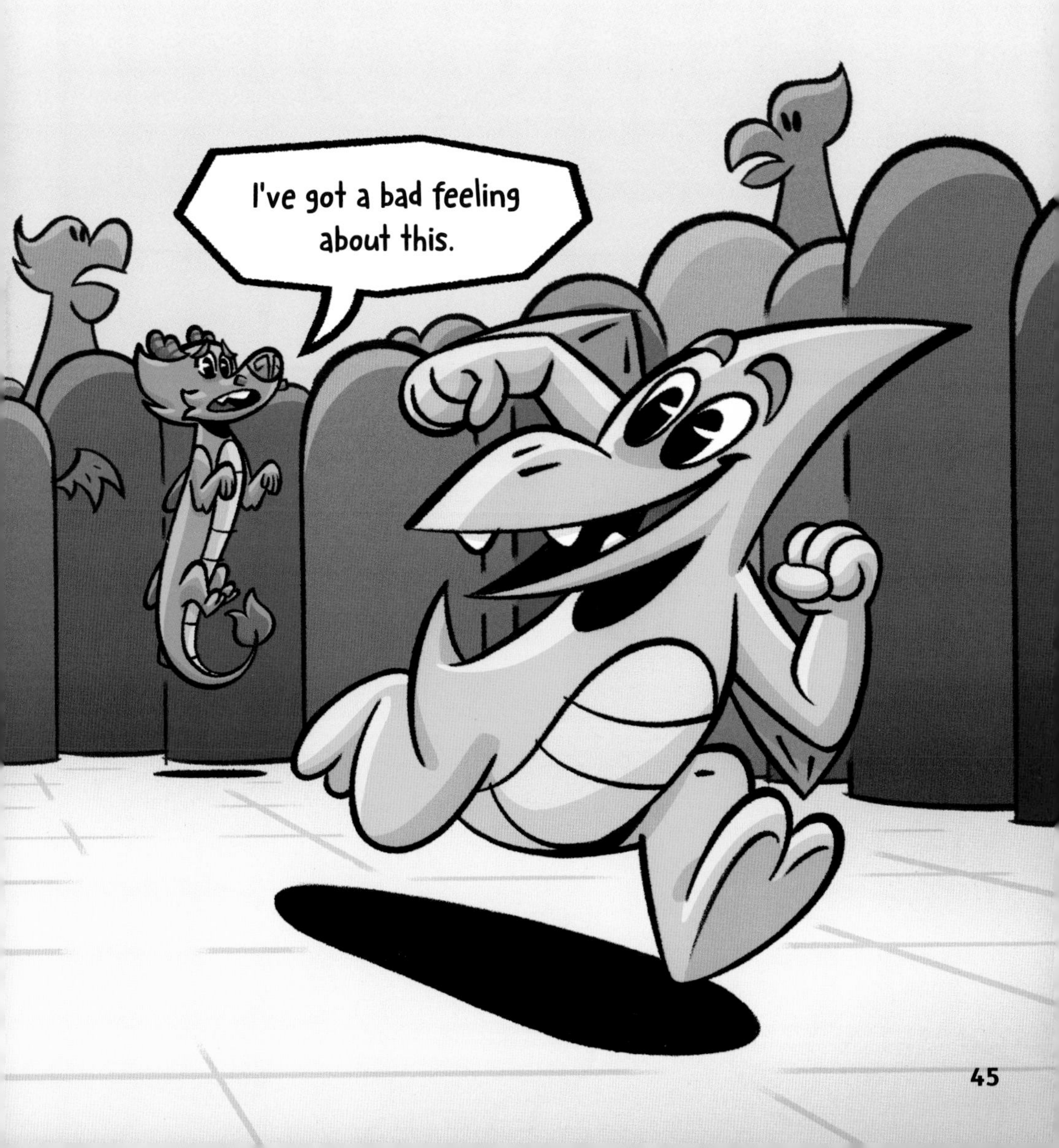
I've got a bad feeling about this.

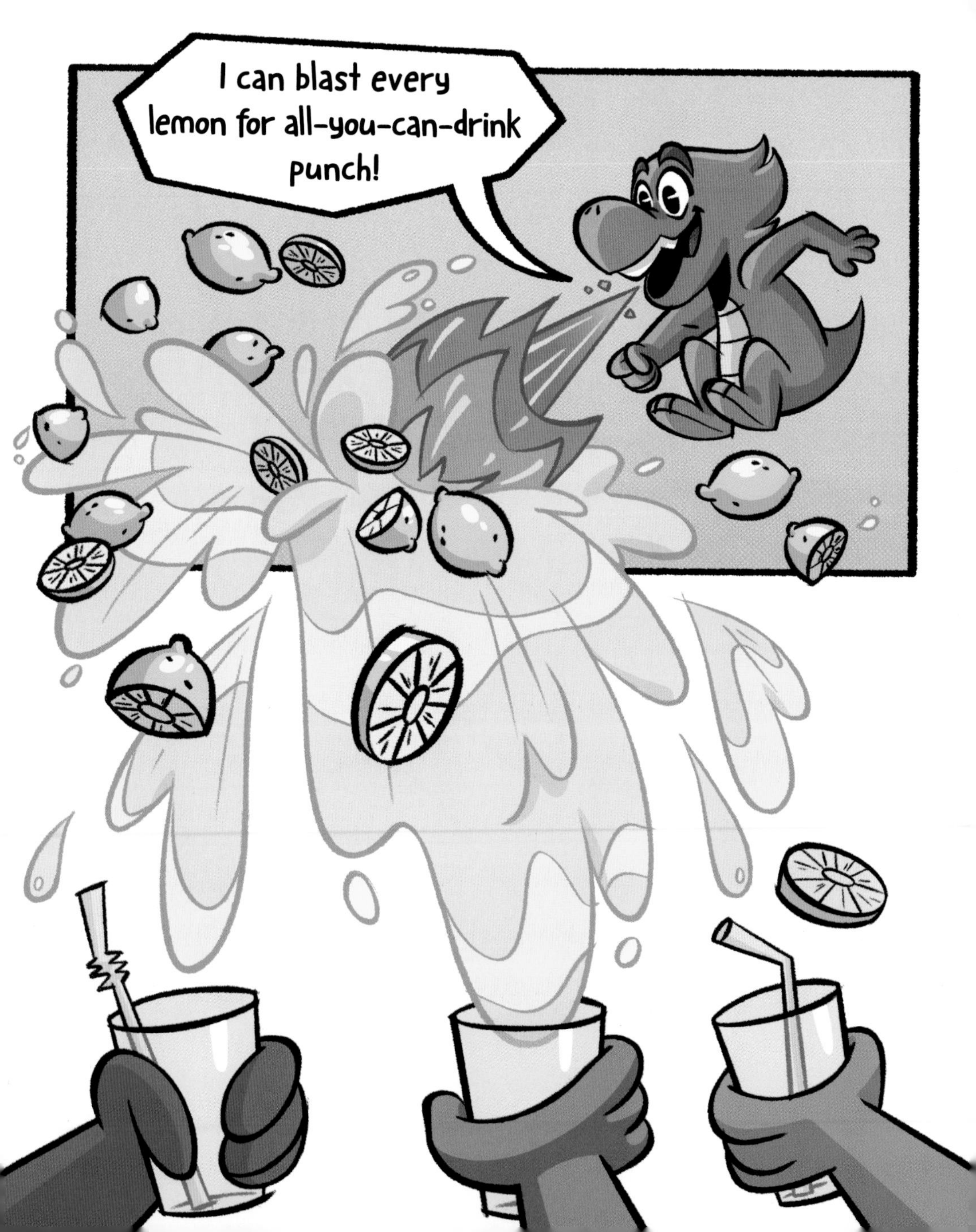
I can blast every lemon for all-you-can-drink punch!

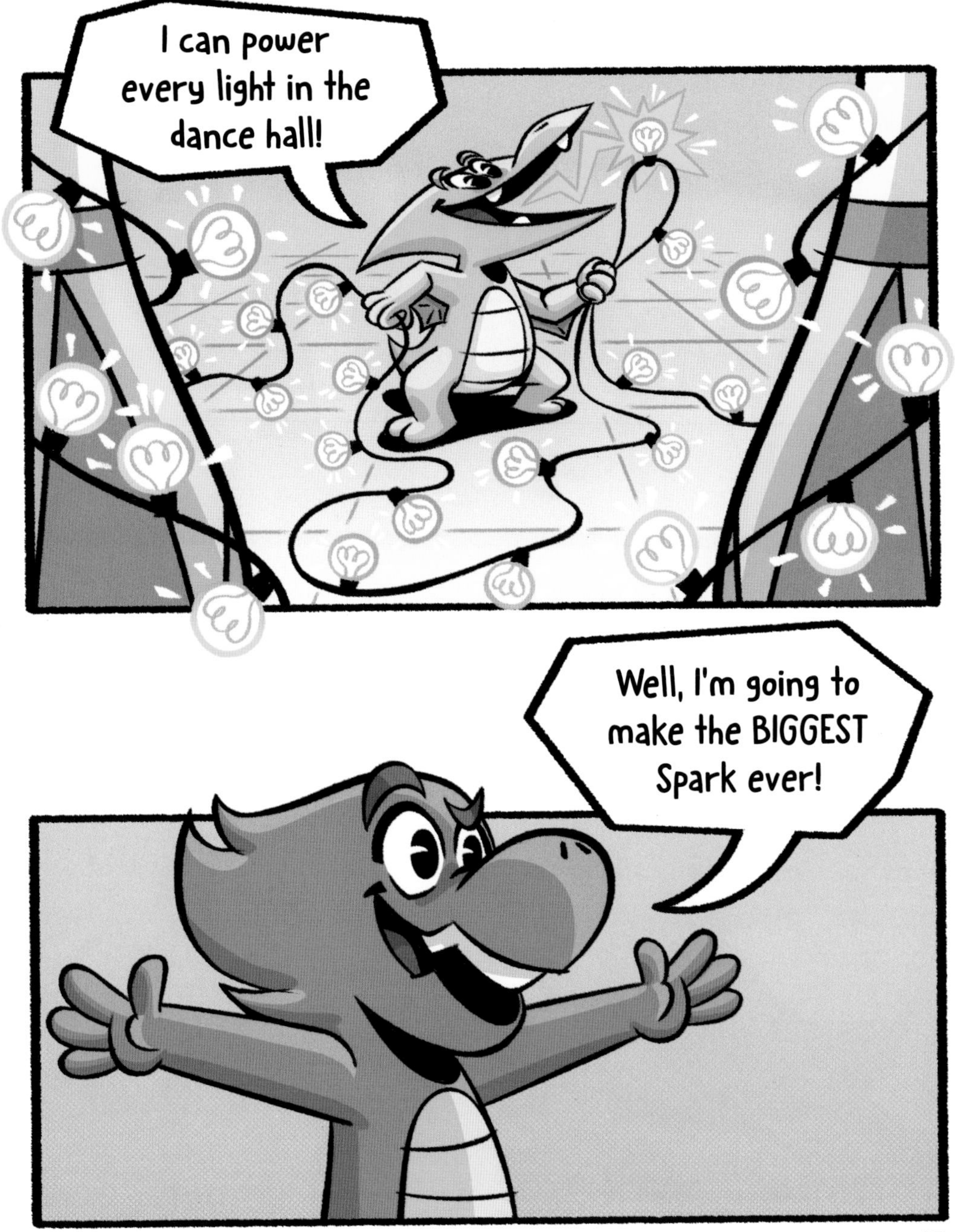
I can power every light in the dance hall!
Well, I'm going to make the BIGGEST Spark ever!

Neither Drake nor Fizz
would back down!

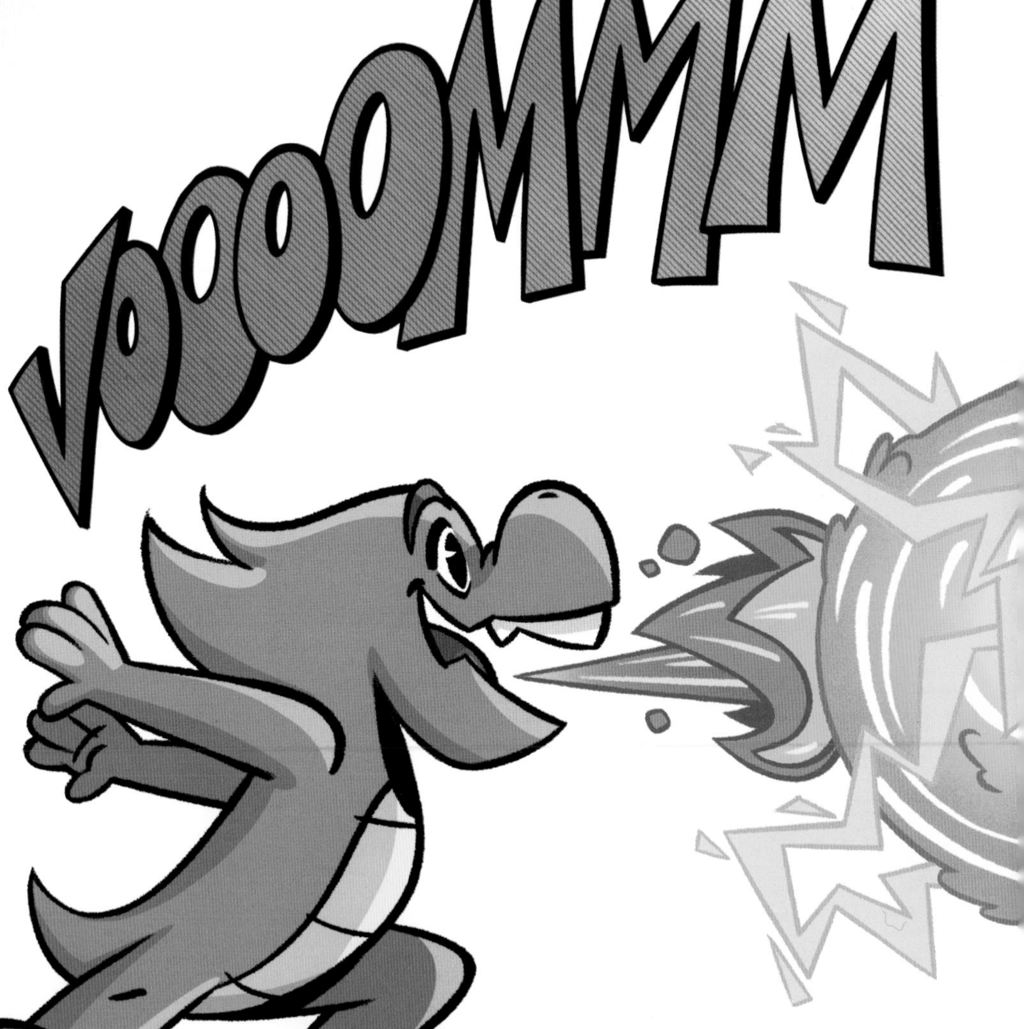
VOOOOMMMM

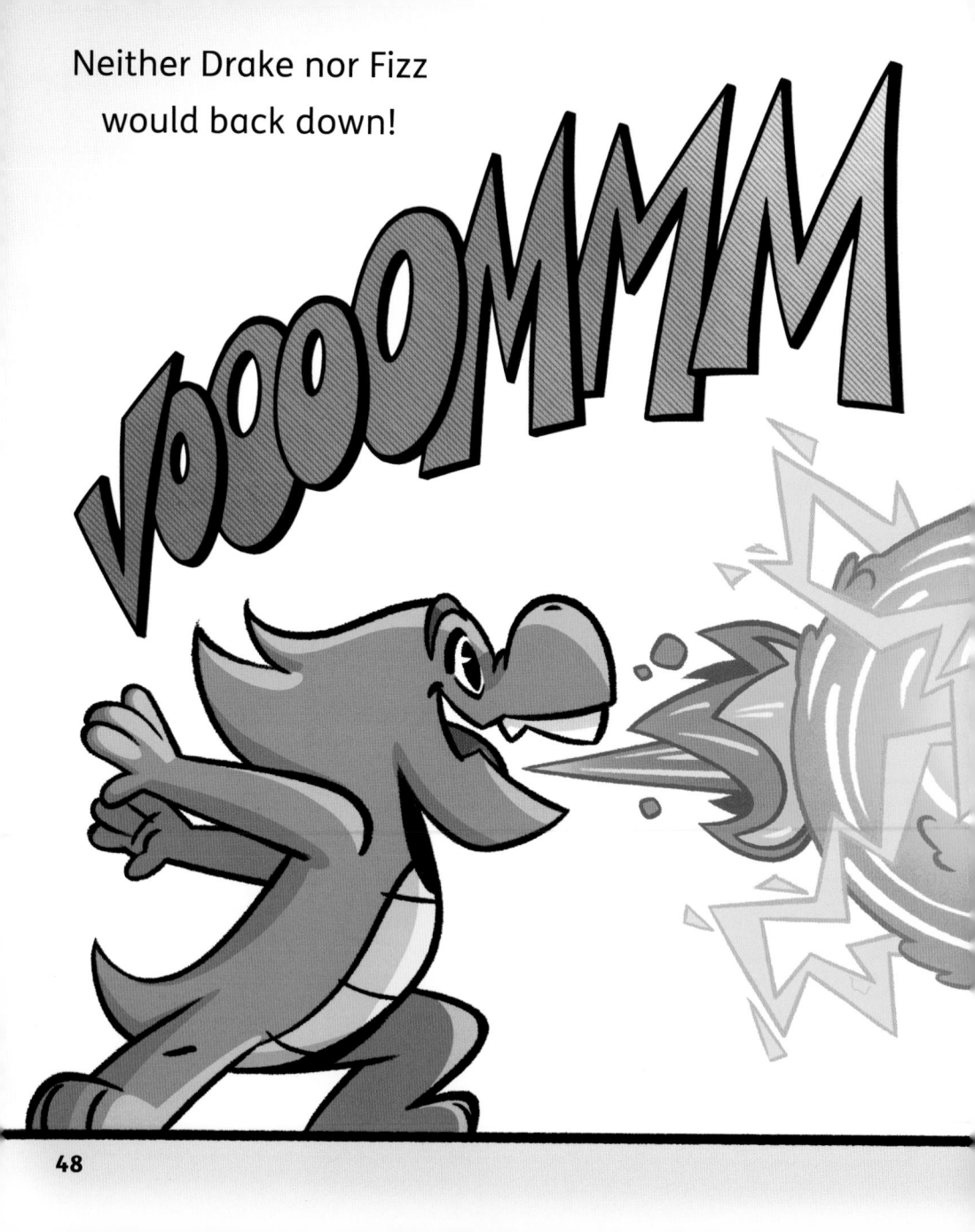

Their Sparks collided!

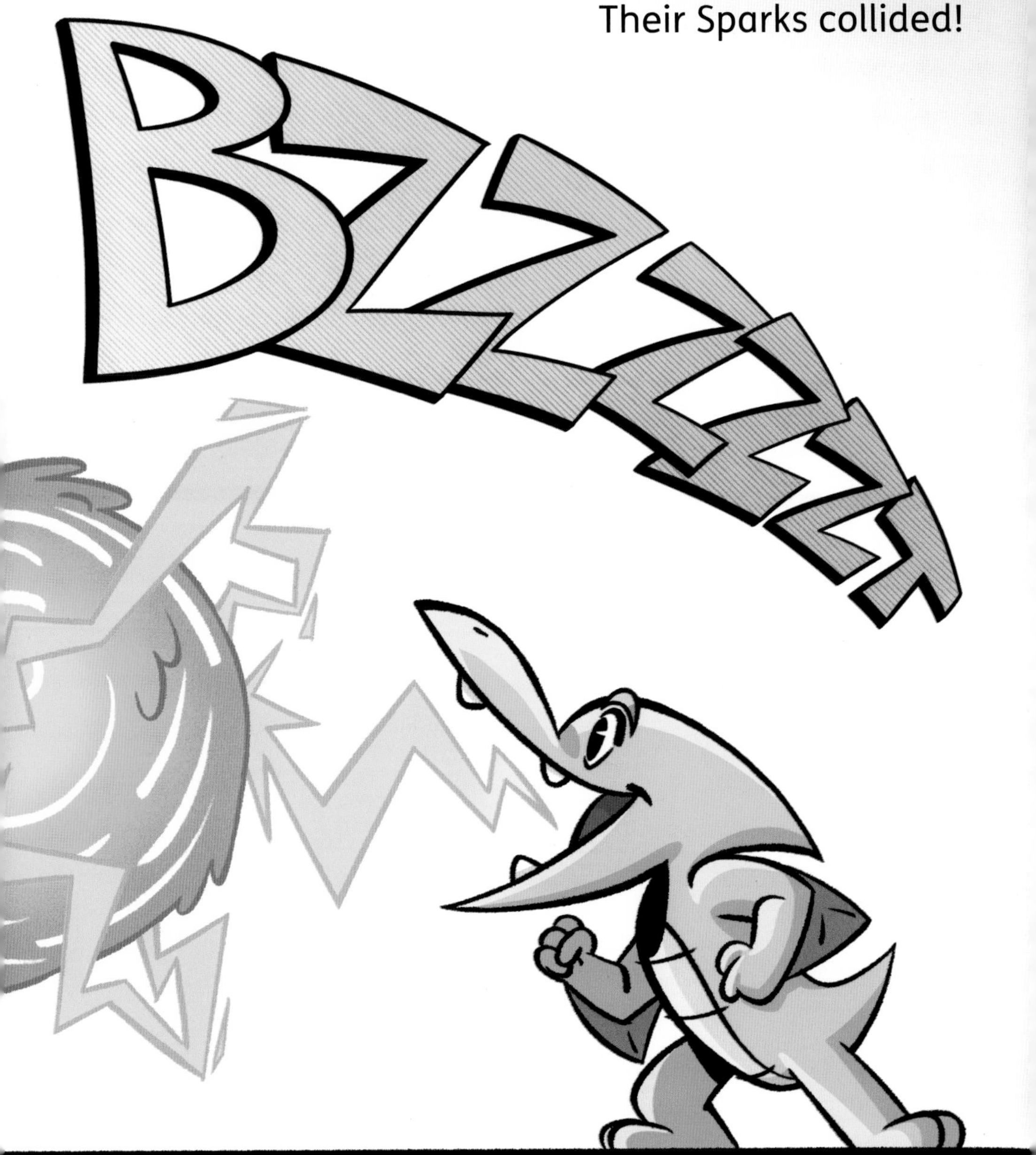
BZZZZZT

Suddenly their Sparks started to bounce all over the room. . . .

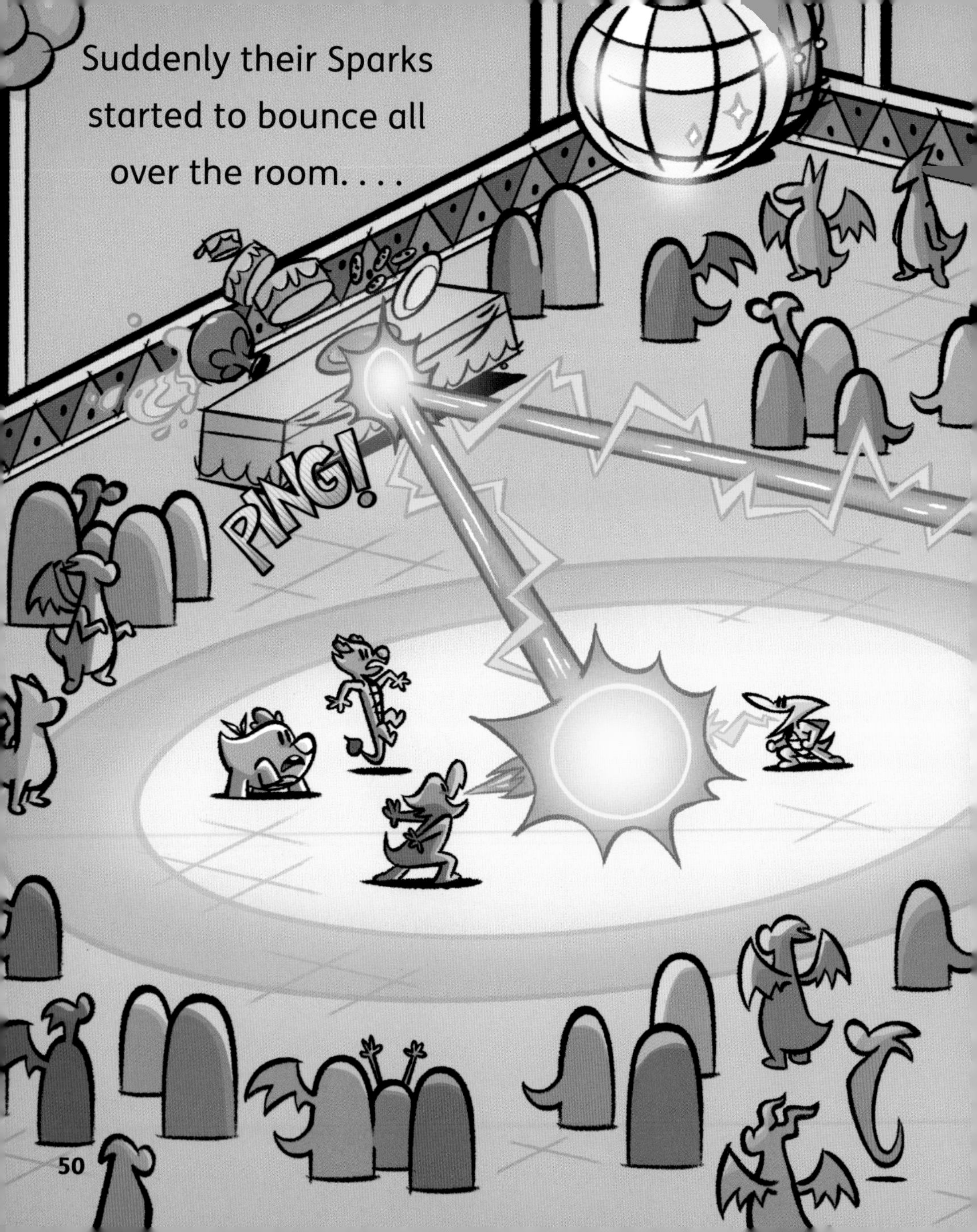
PING!

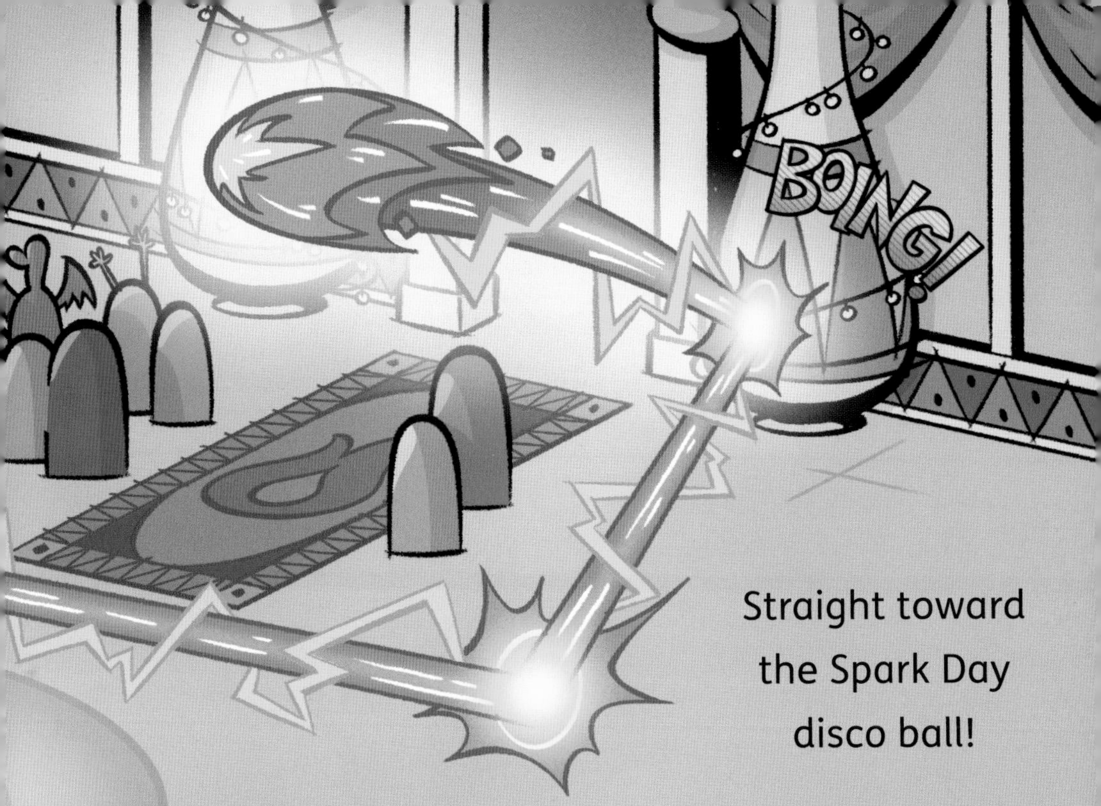
BOING!

Straight toward
the Spark Day
disco ball!

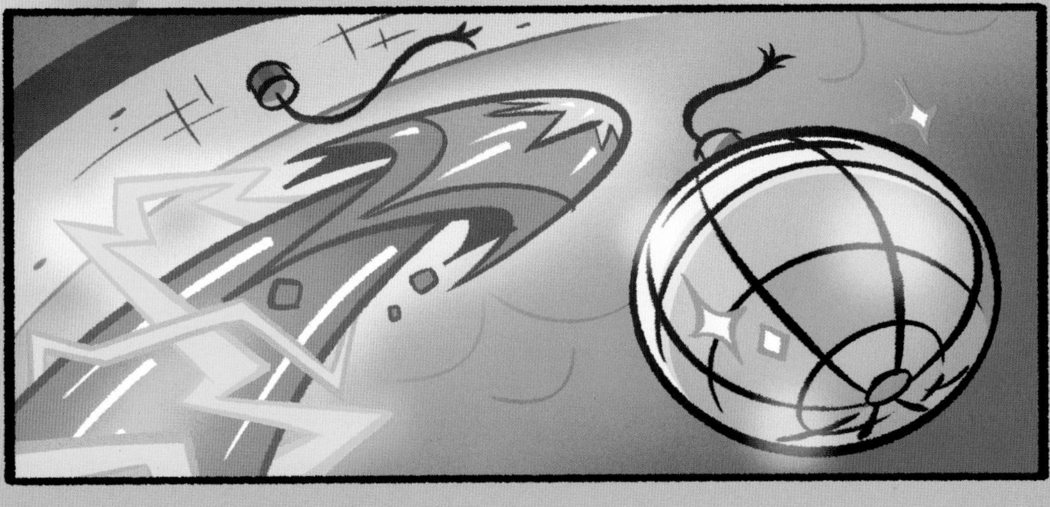

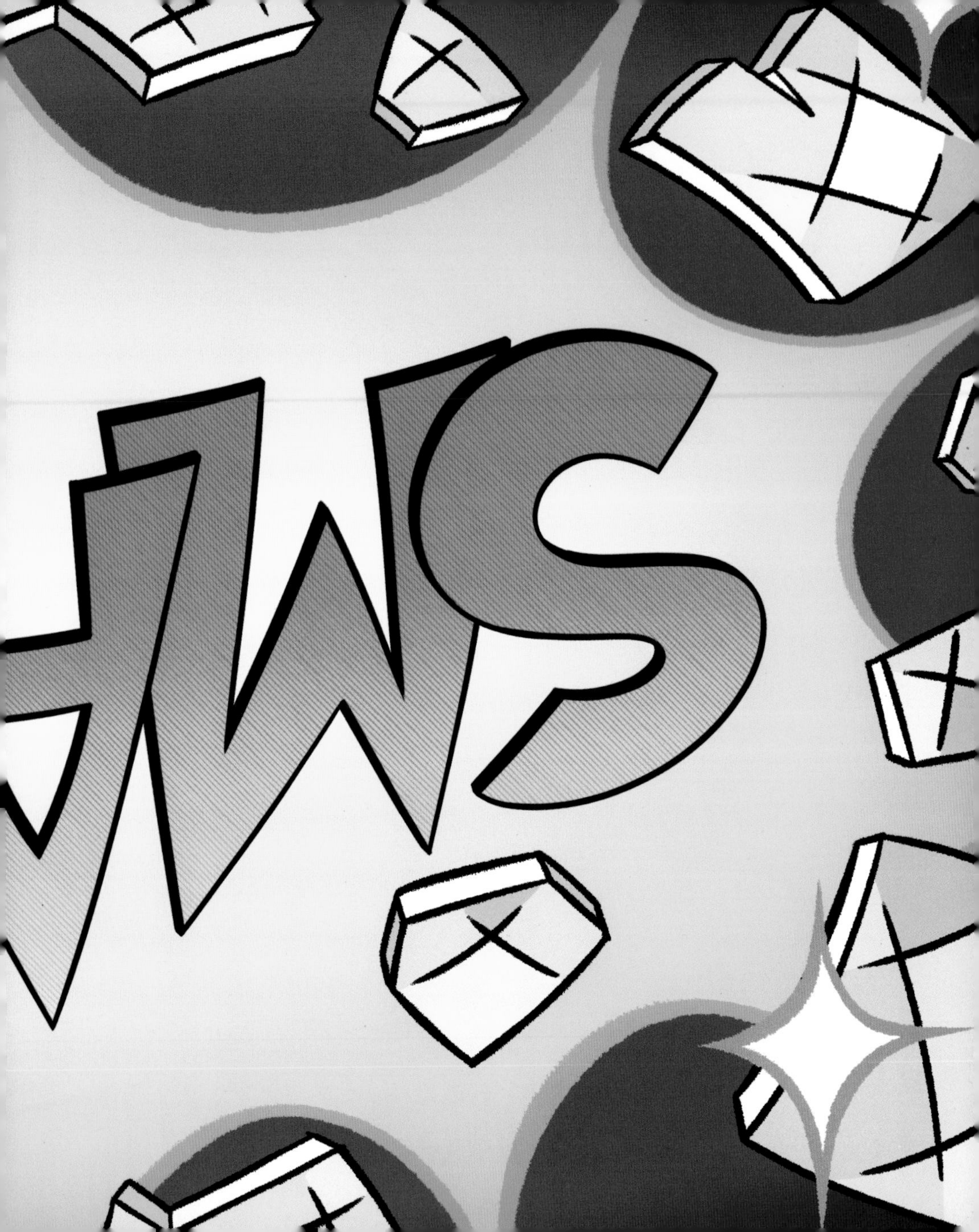
WS

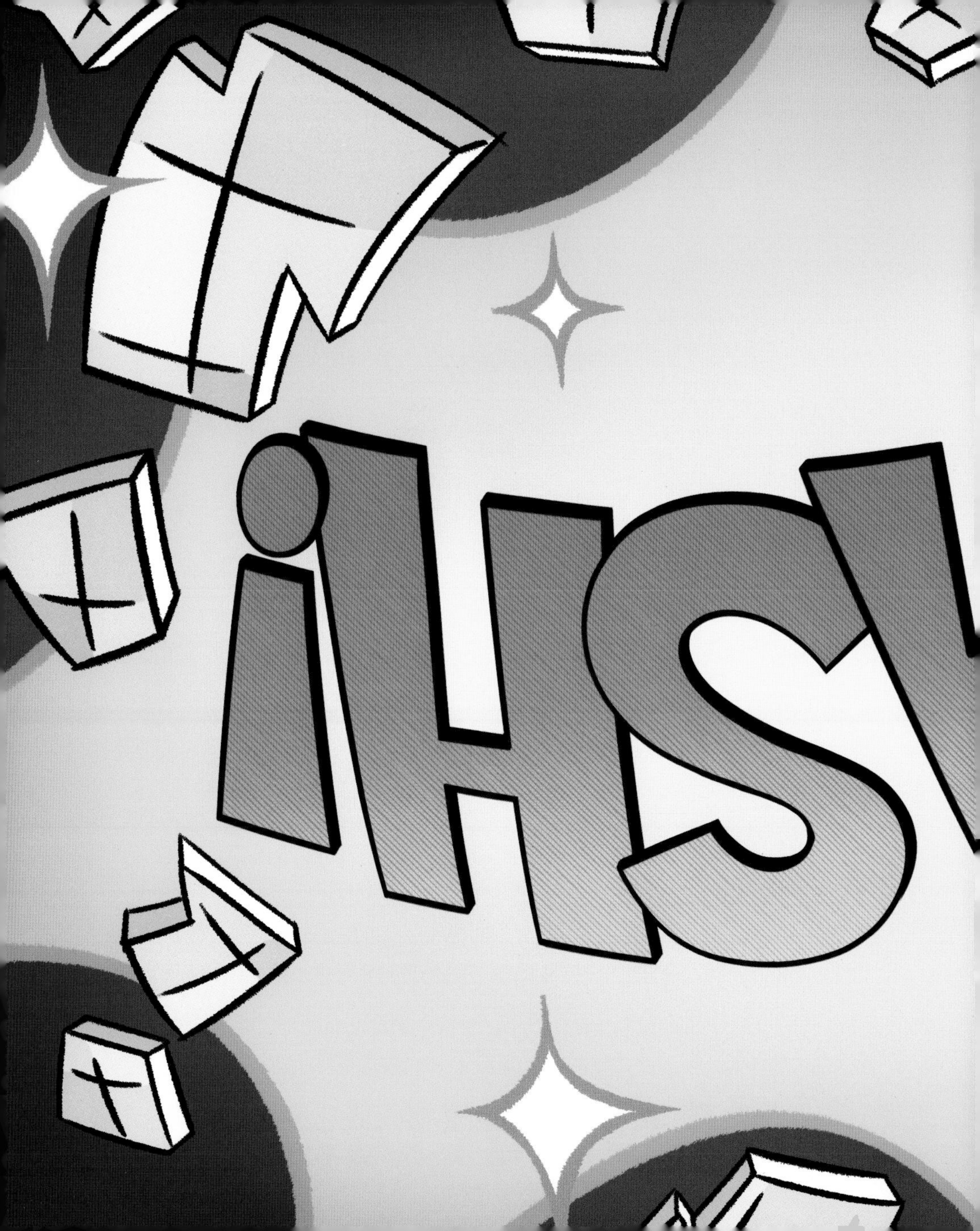

CHAPTER FOUR

No one spoke. No one moved.
Every dragon was shocked.

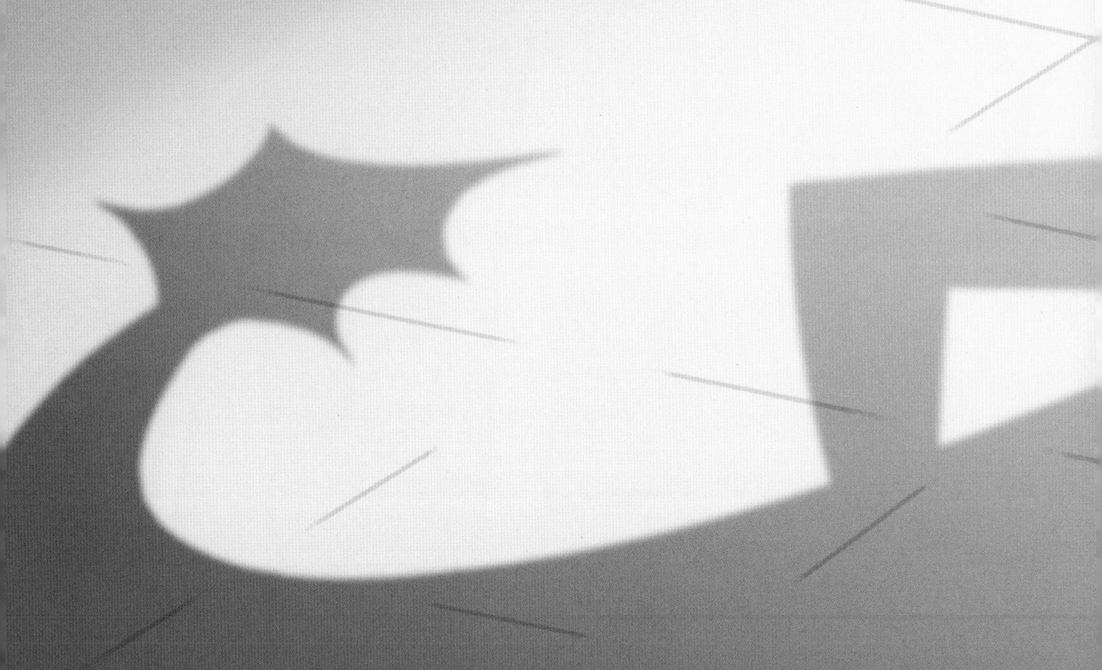

The legendary disco ball was ruined.

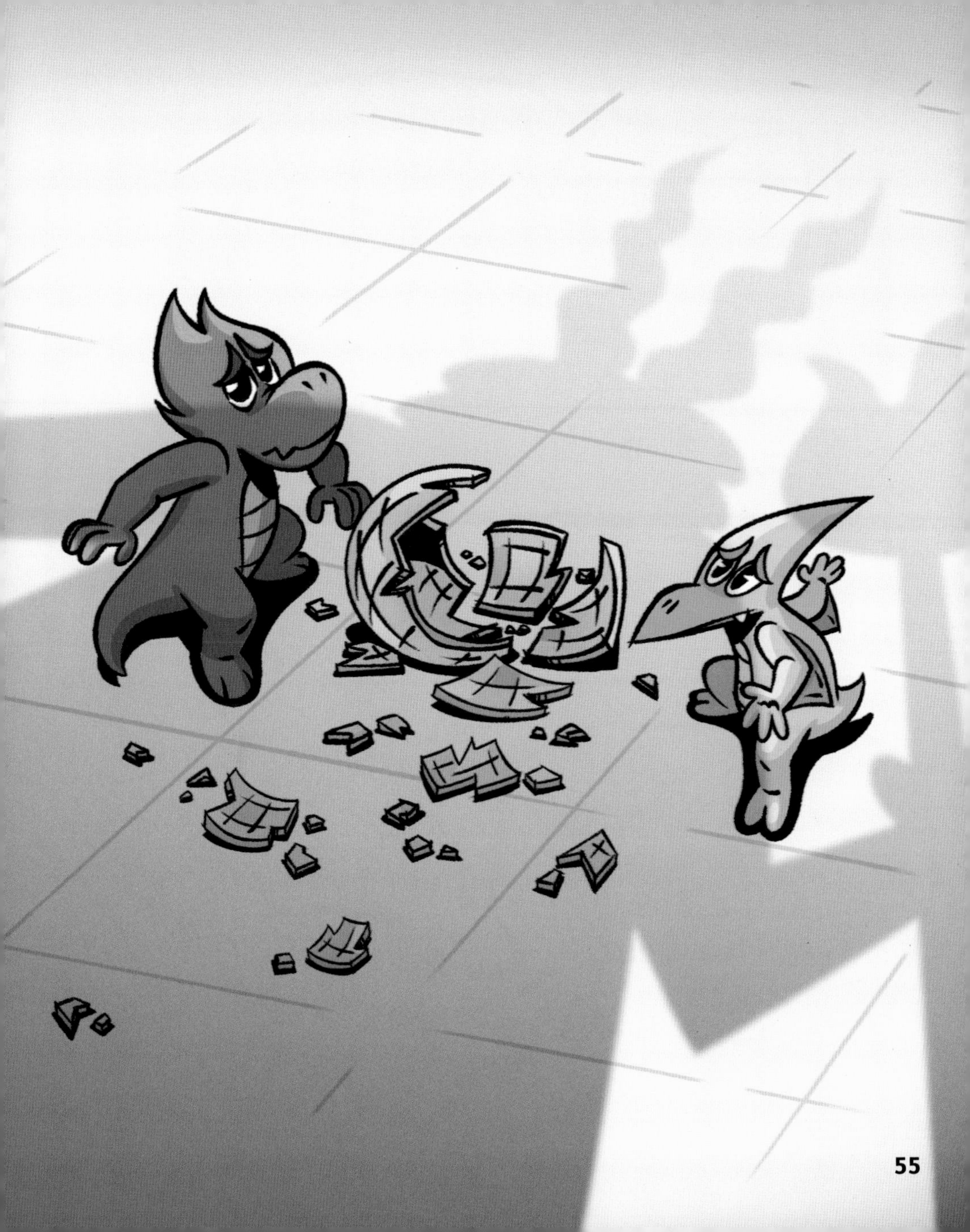

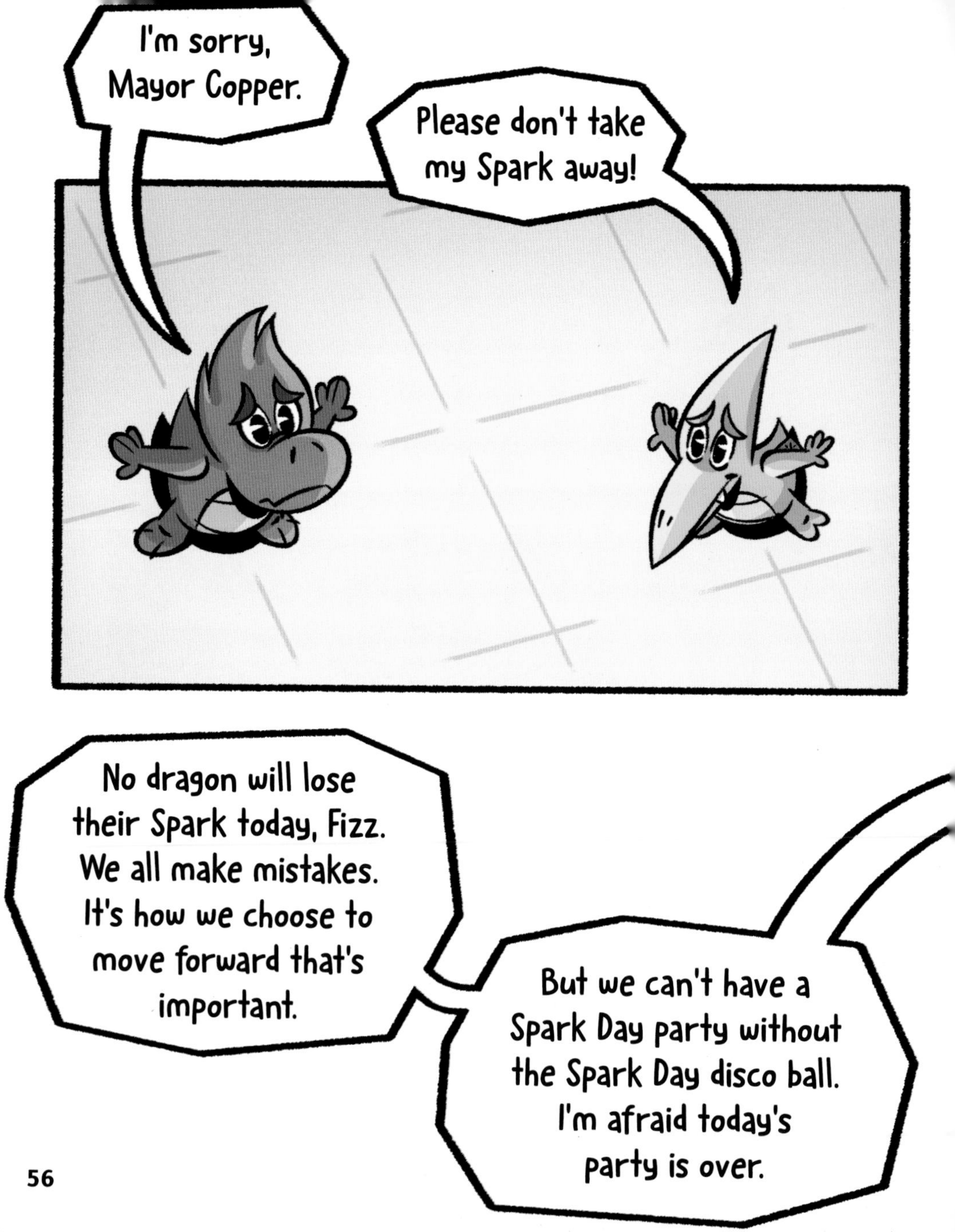
I'm sorry, Mayor Copper.
Please don't take my Spark away!
No dragon will lose their Spark today, Fizz. We all make mistakes. It's how we choose to move forward that's important.
But we can't have a Spark Day party without the Spark Day disco ball. I'm afraid today's party is over.

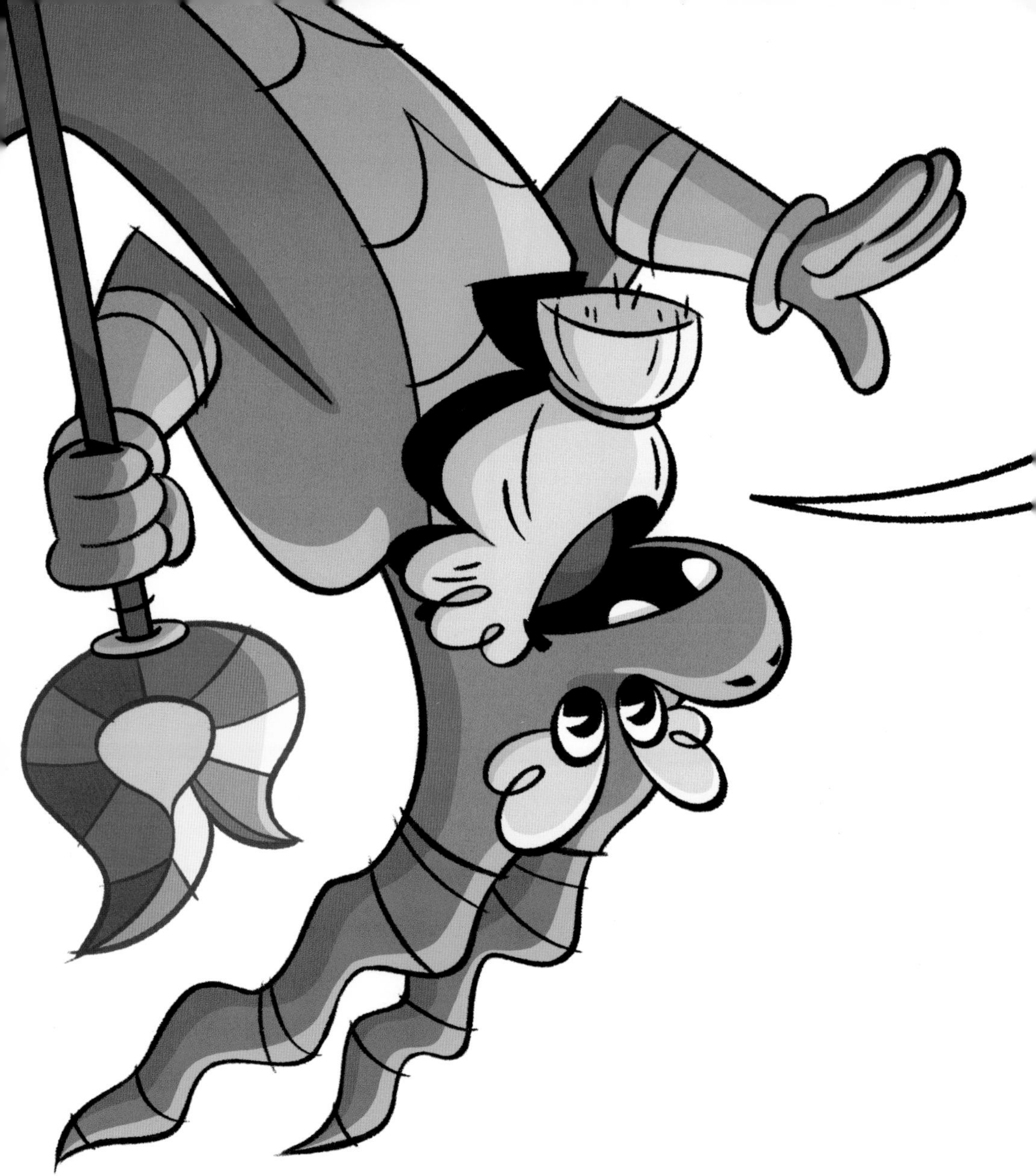

Almost all the dragons left the party. Only Drake, Runa, Li, and Fizz stayed behind.

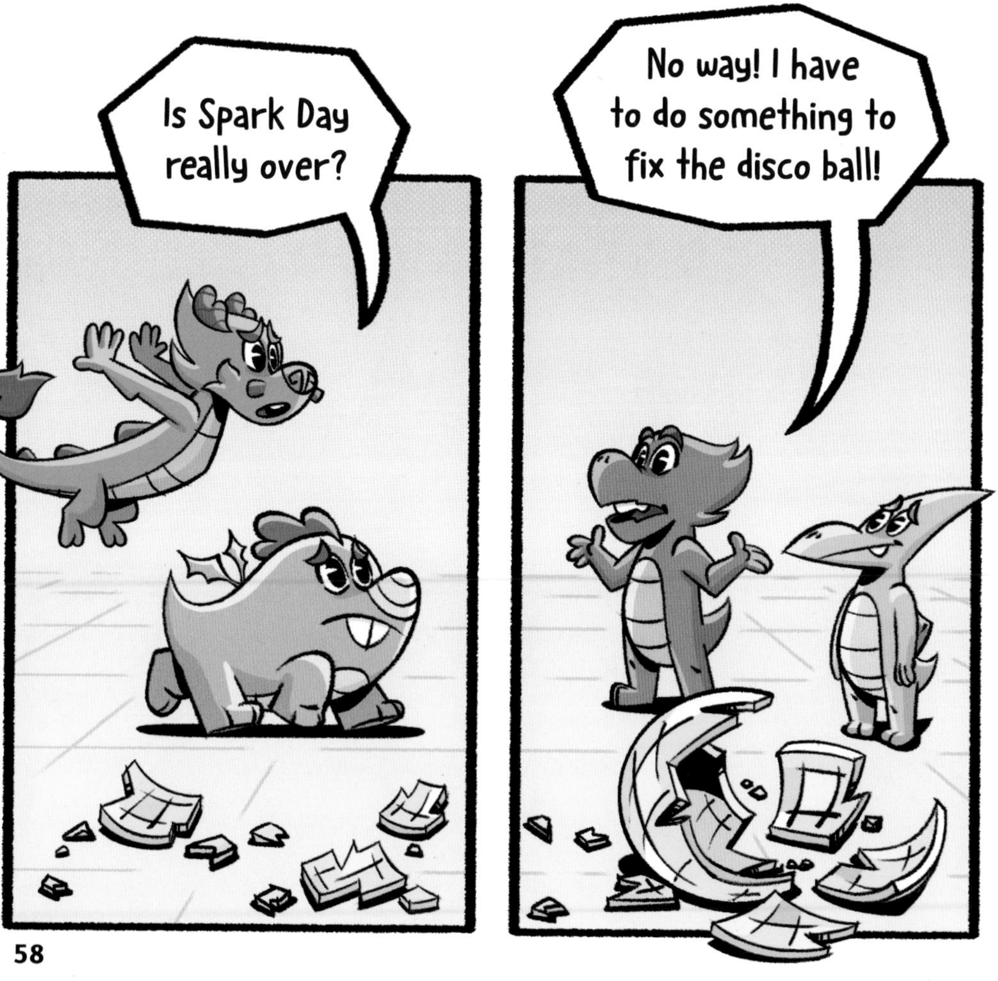
Is Spark Day really over?
No way! I have to do something to fix the disco ball!

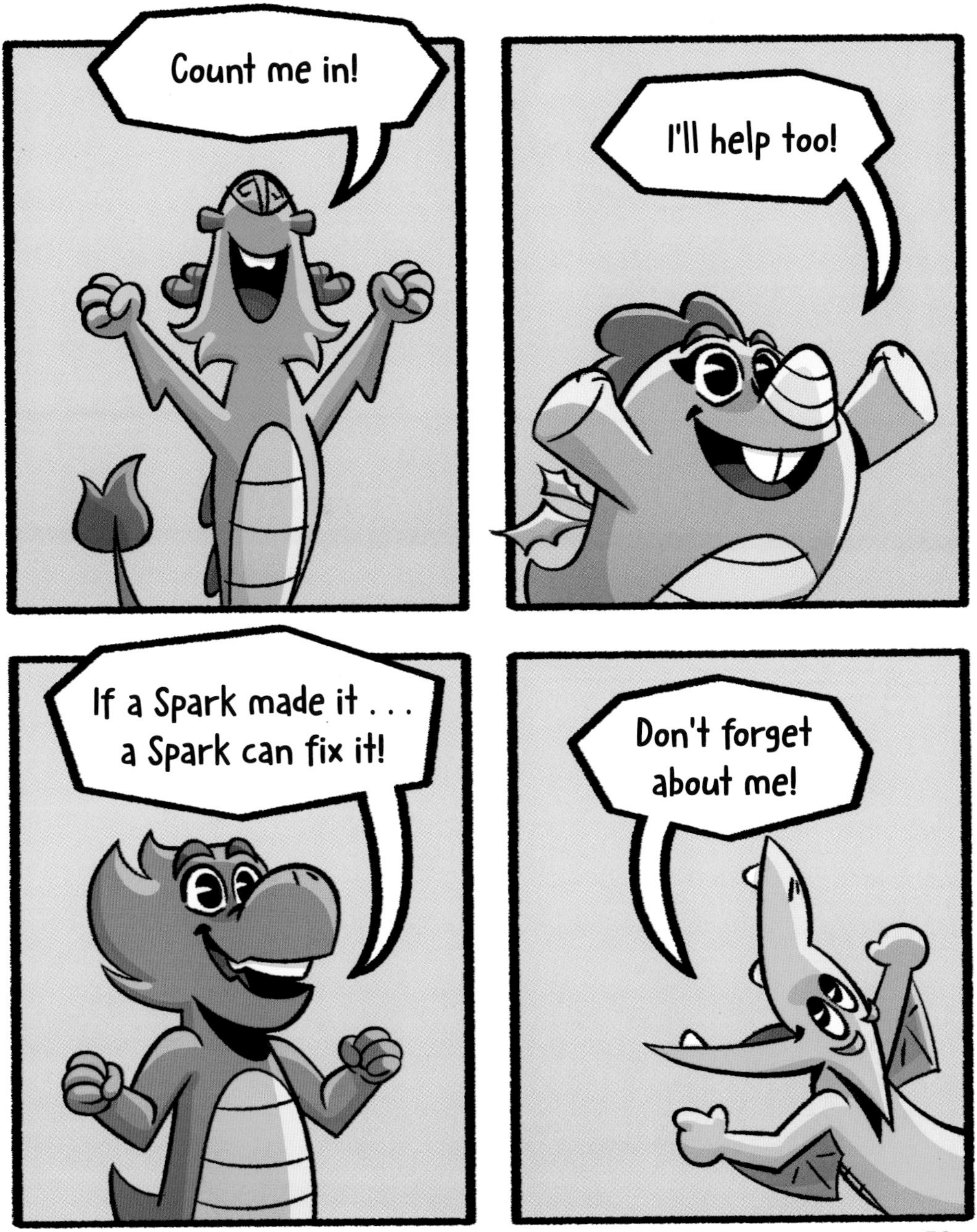
Count me in!
I'll help too!
If a Spark made it . . .
a Spark can fix it!
Don't forget
about me!

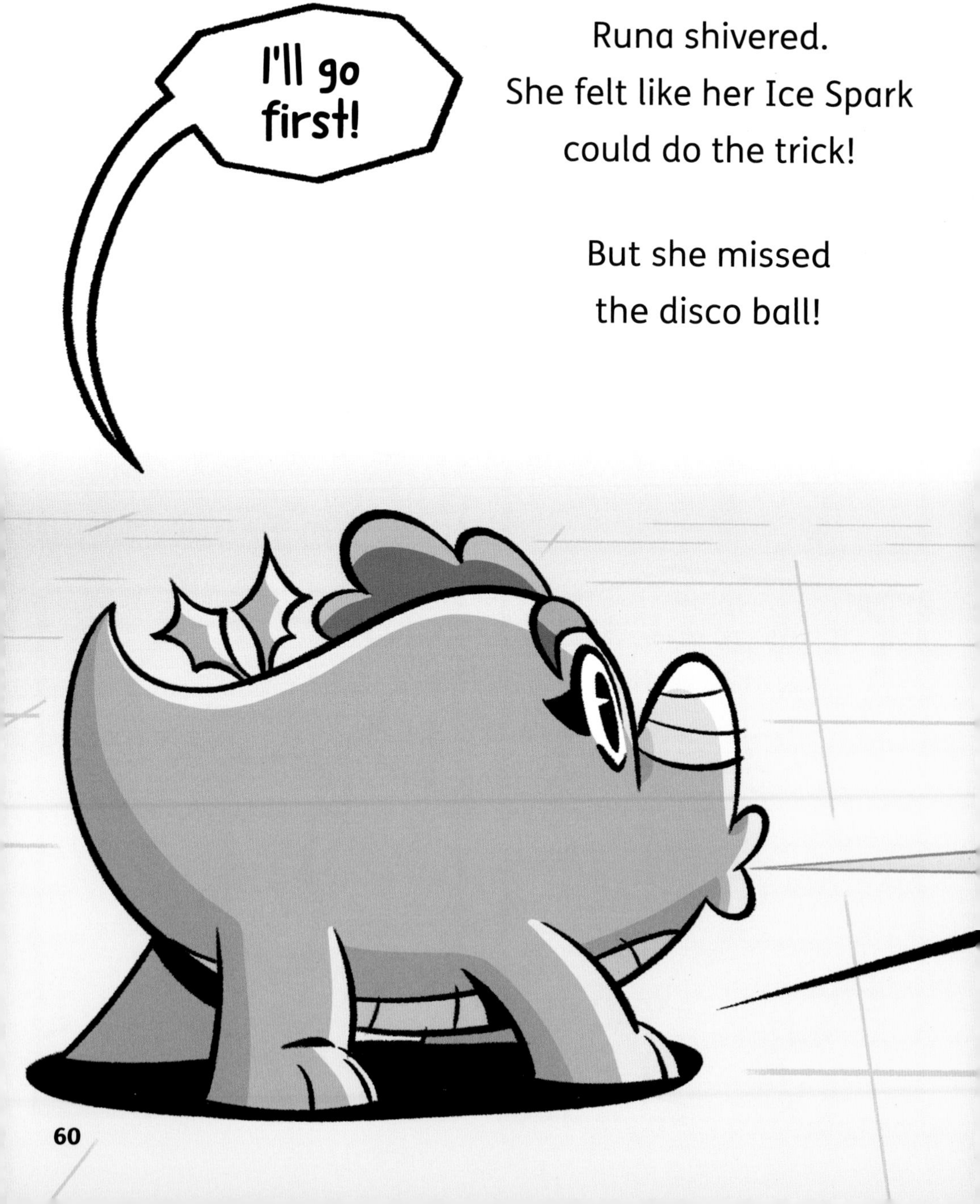
I'll go first!

Runa shivered.
She felt like her Ice Spark
could do the trick!

But she missed
the disco ball!

Runa accidentally made the floor an ice-skating rink.

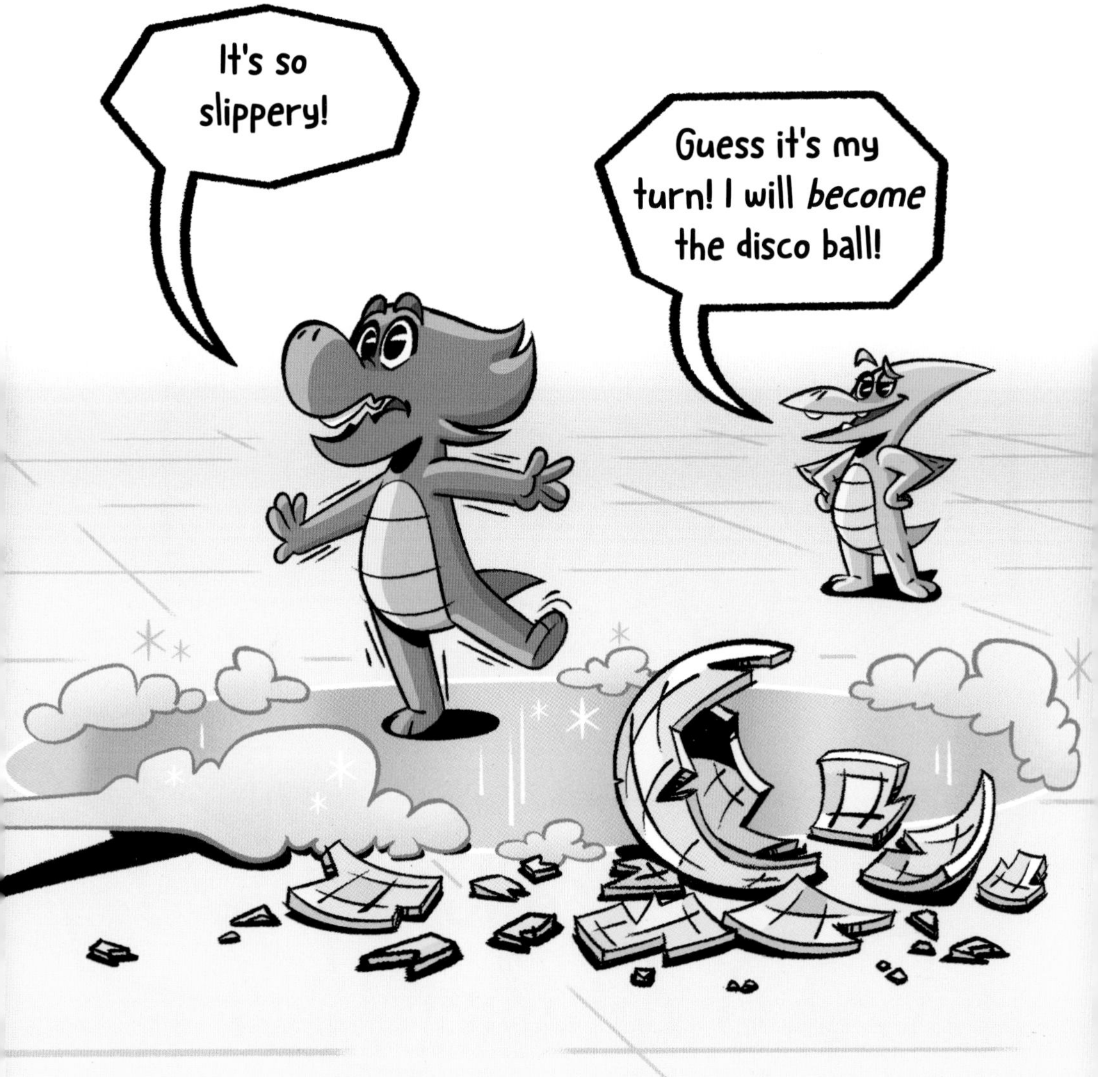
It's so slippery!
Guess it's my turn! I will *become* the disco ball!

Fizz held his breath as his Lightning Spark started to make his tummy glow.

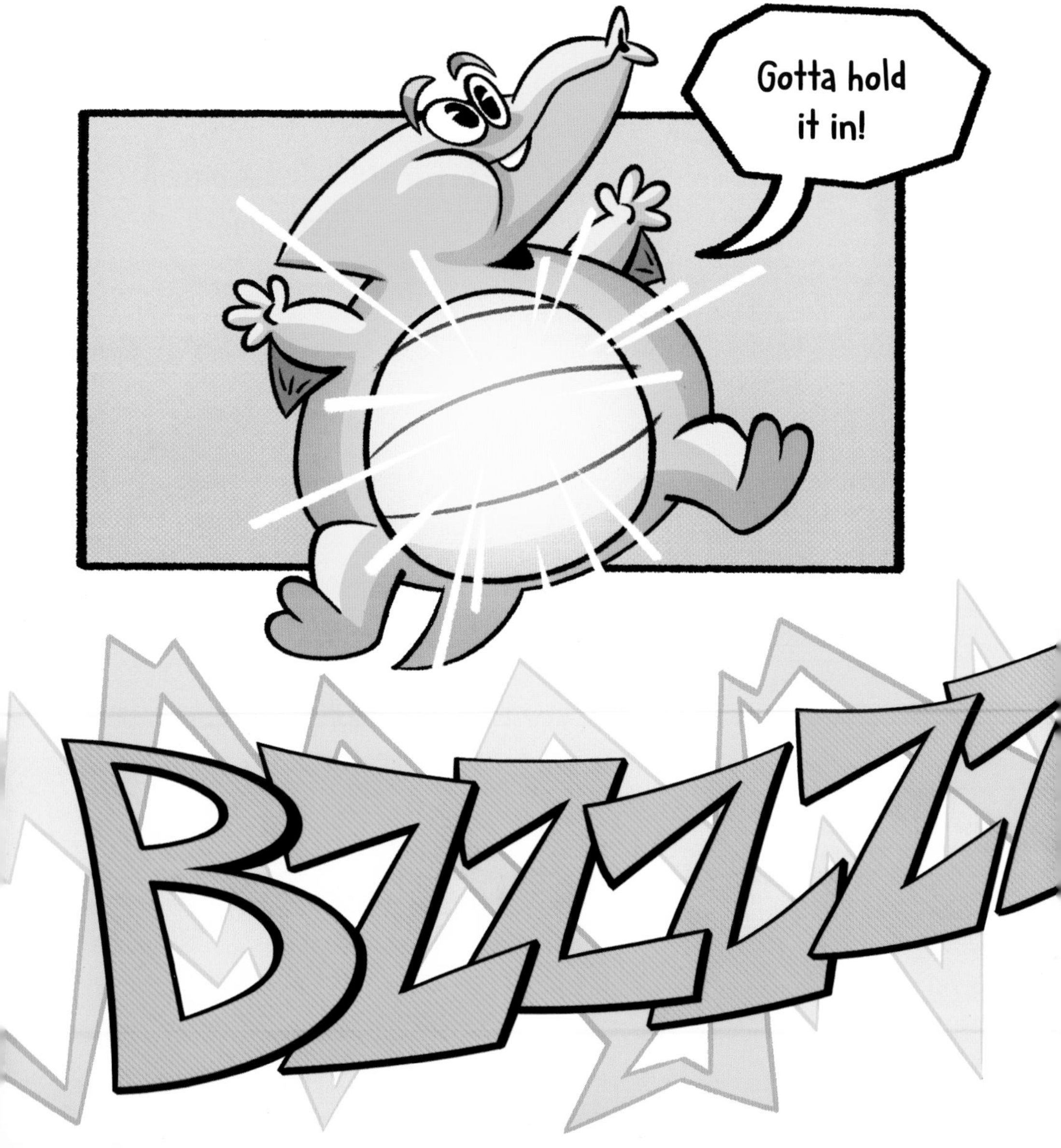
Gotta hold it in!
BZZZZ

But Fizz couldn't
hold it in.

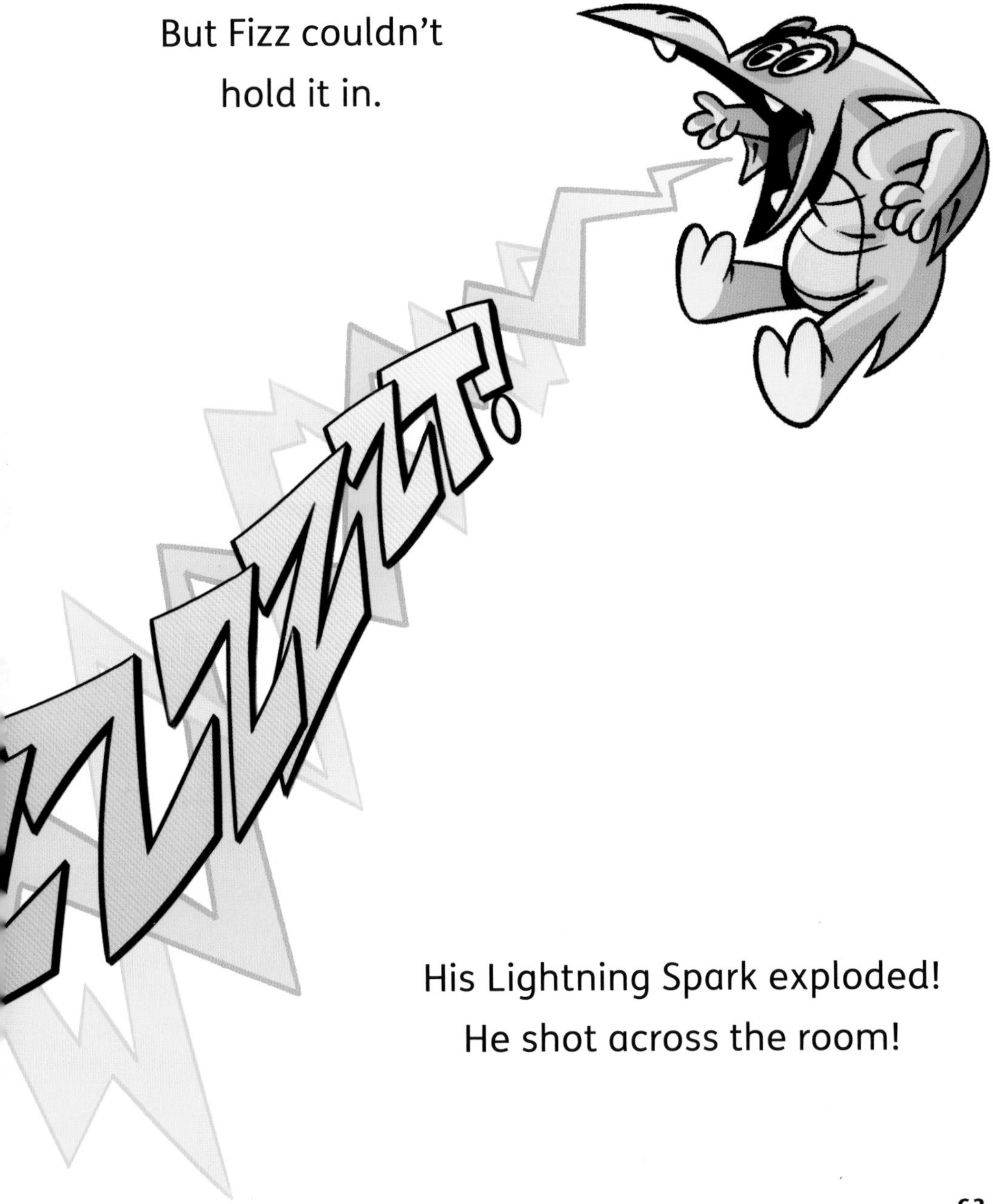
ZZZZT!

His Lightning Spark exploded!
He shot across the room!

And landed butt-first in a
sparkly sprinkle cake!

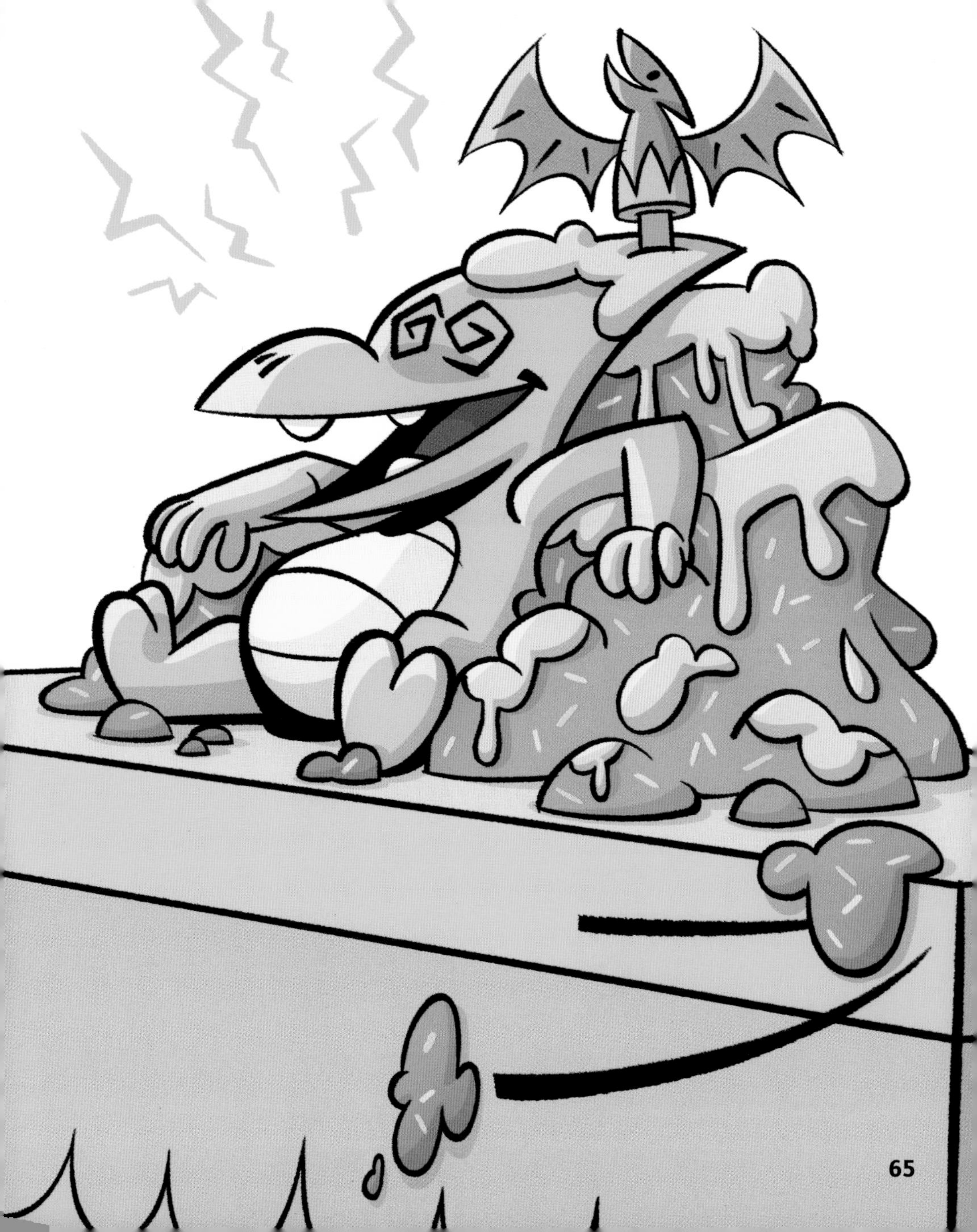

CHAPTER FIVE

The ballroom looked worse than before, if that was even possible.

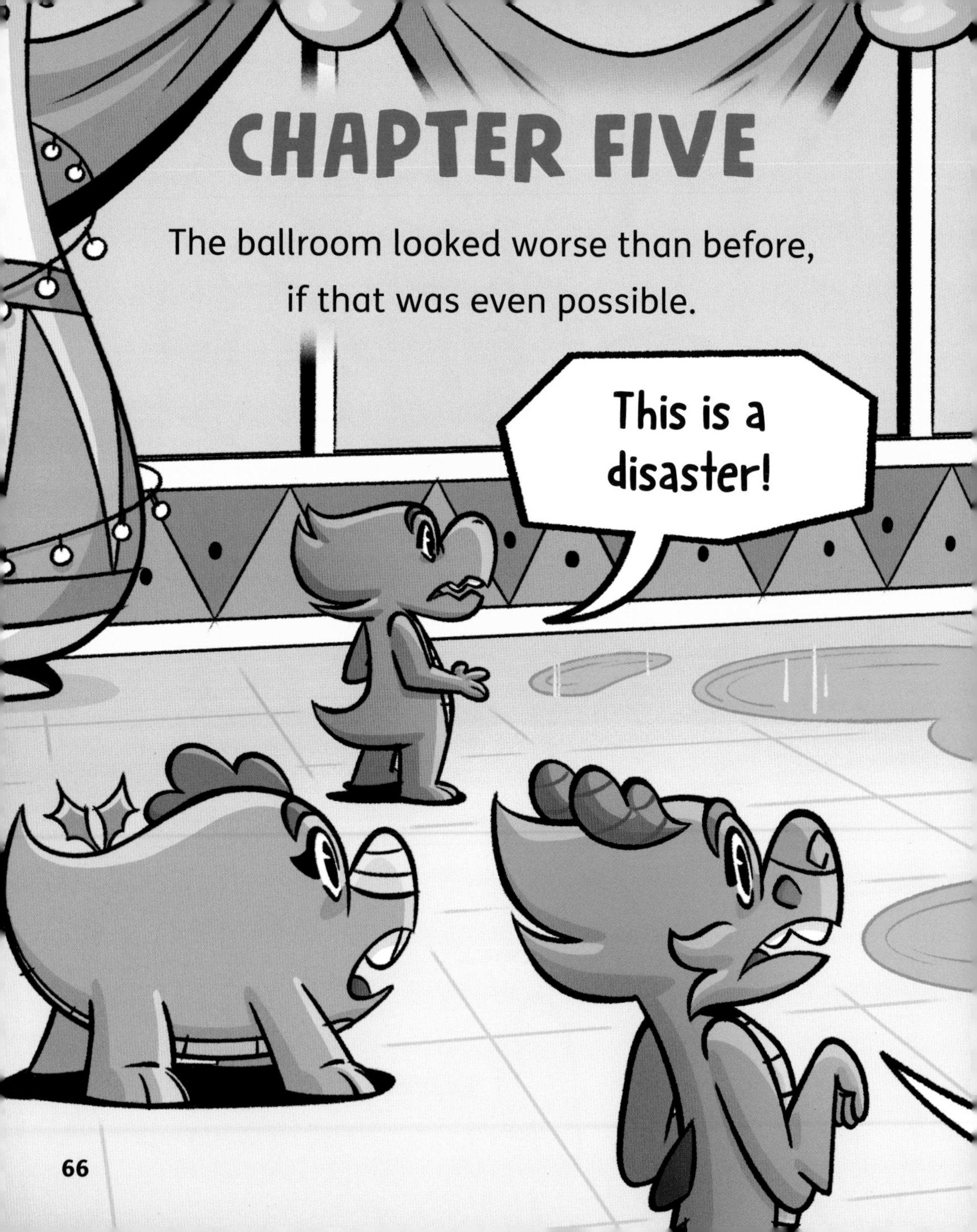
This is a disaster!

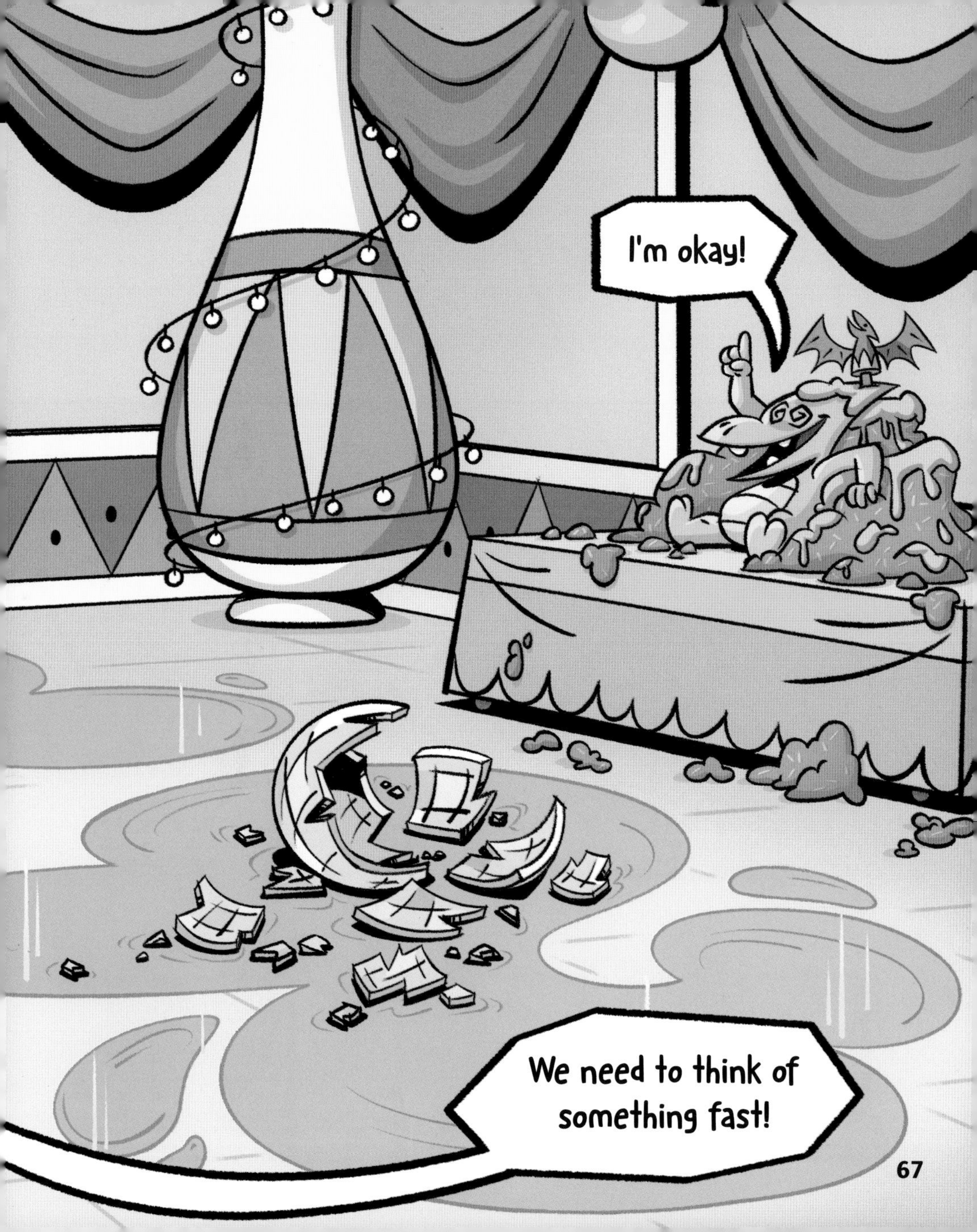
I'm okay!
We need to think of something fast!

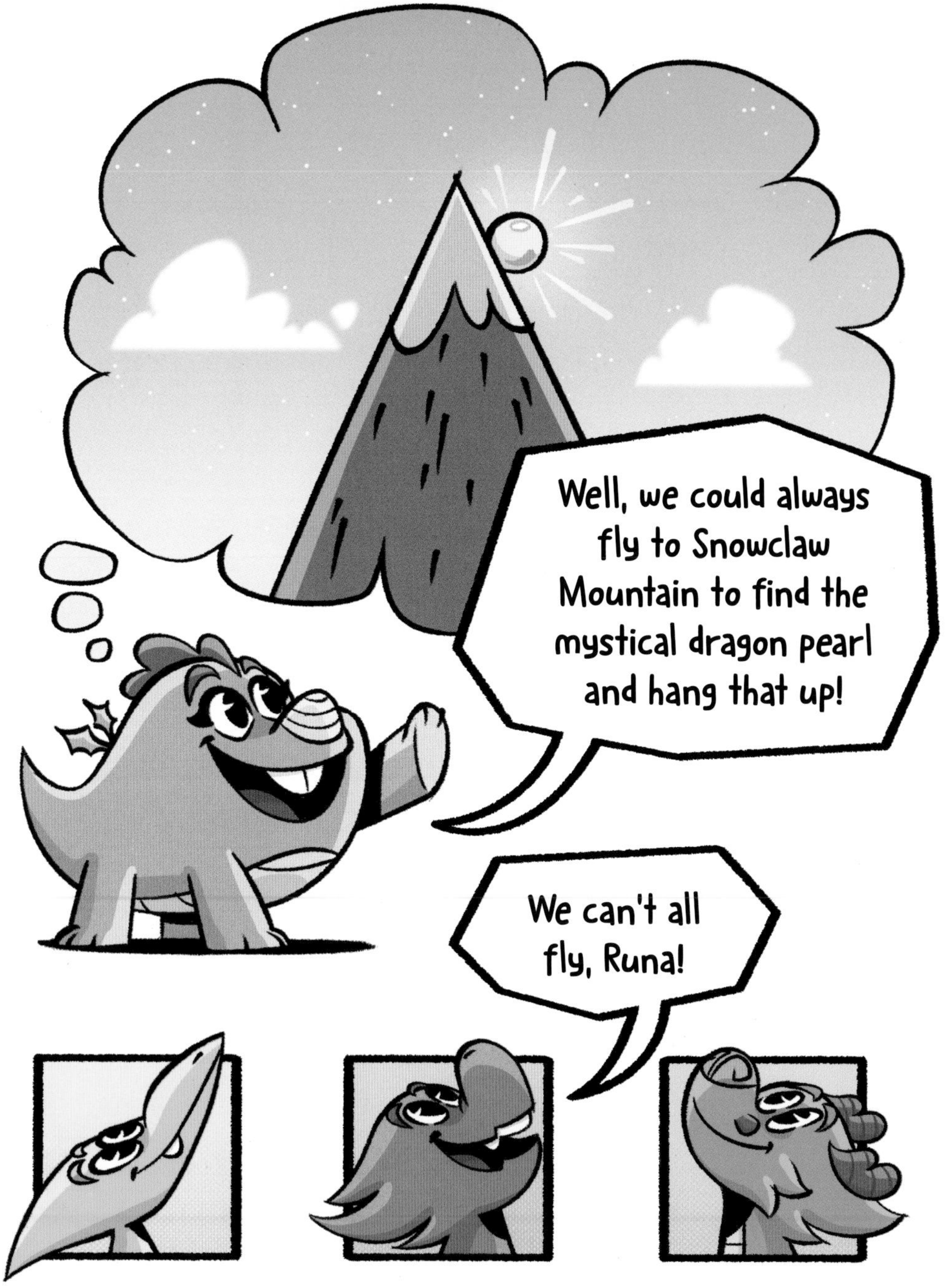
Well, we could always fly to Snowclaw Mountain to find the mystical dragon pearl and hang that up!
We can't all fly, Runa!

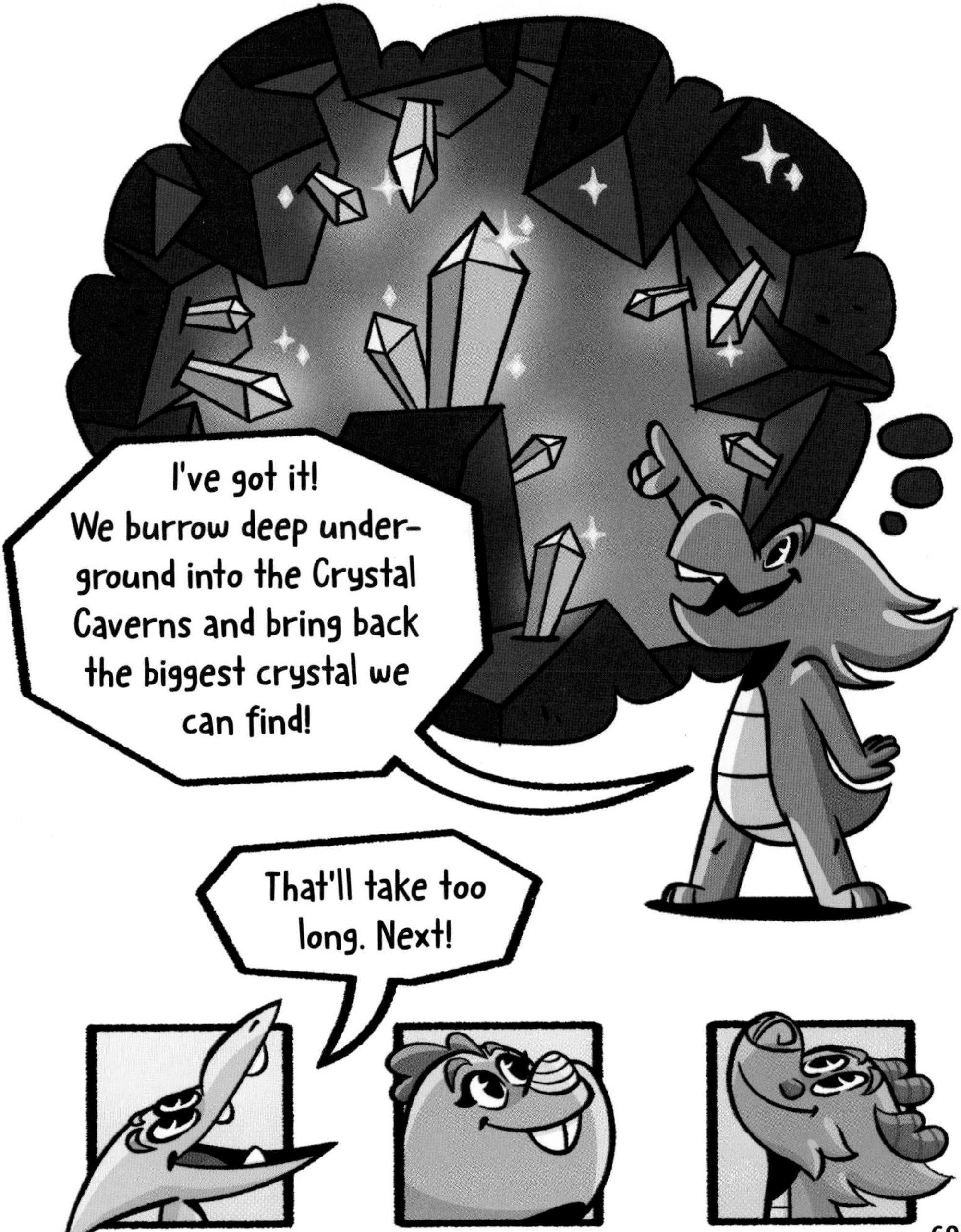
I've got it!
We burrow deep under-ground into the Crystal Caverns and bring back the biggest crystal we can find!
That'll take too long. Next!

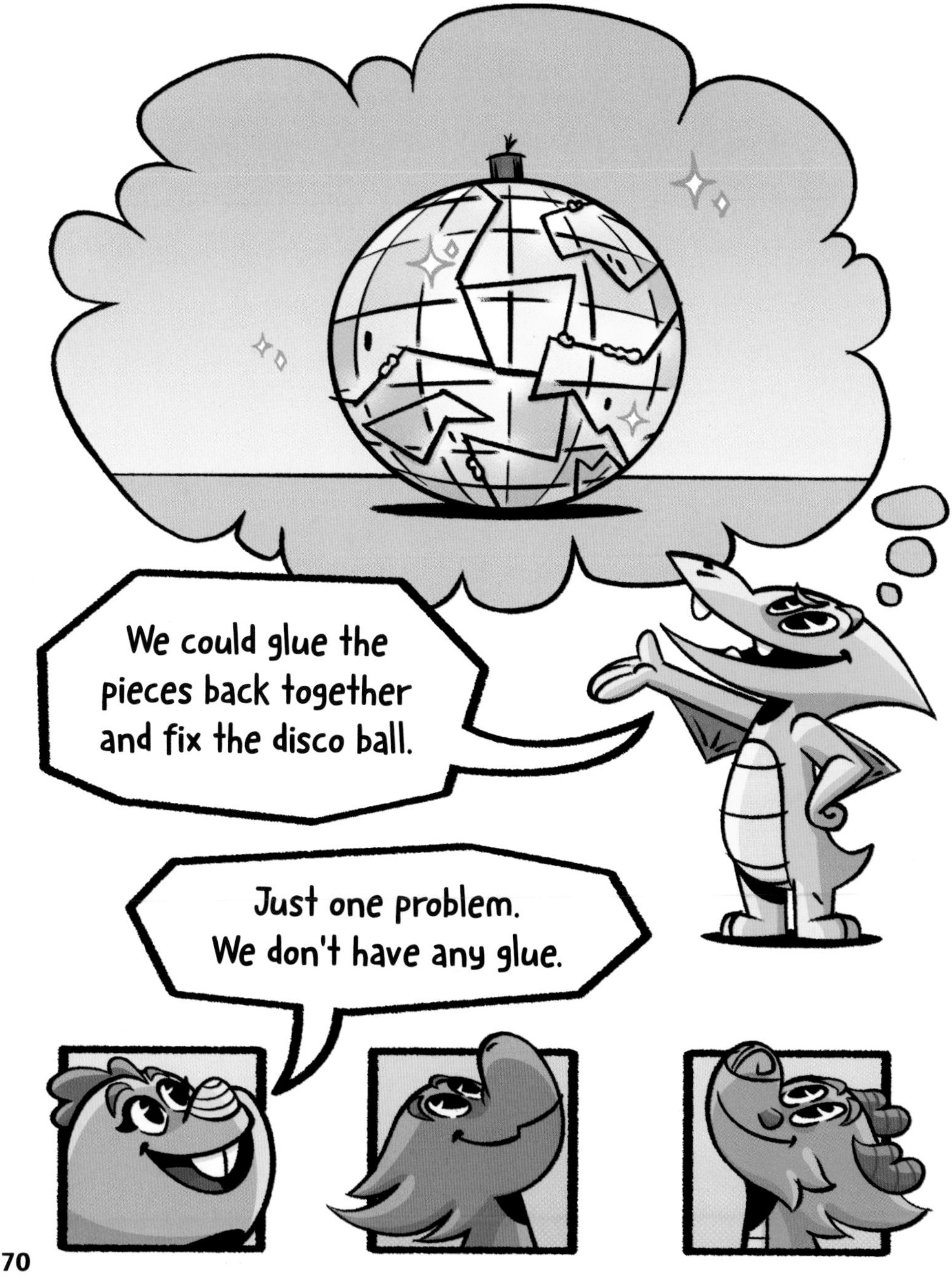
We could glue the pieces back together and fix the disco ball.
Just one problem. We don't have any glue.

Li pulled out a bottle of sticky glue!

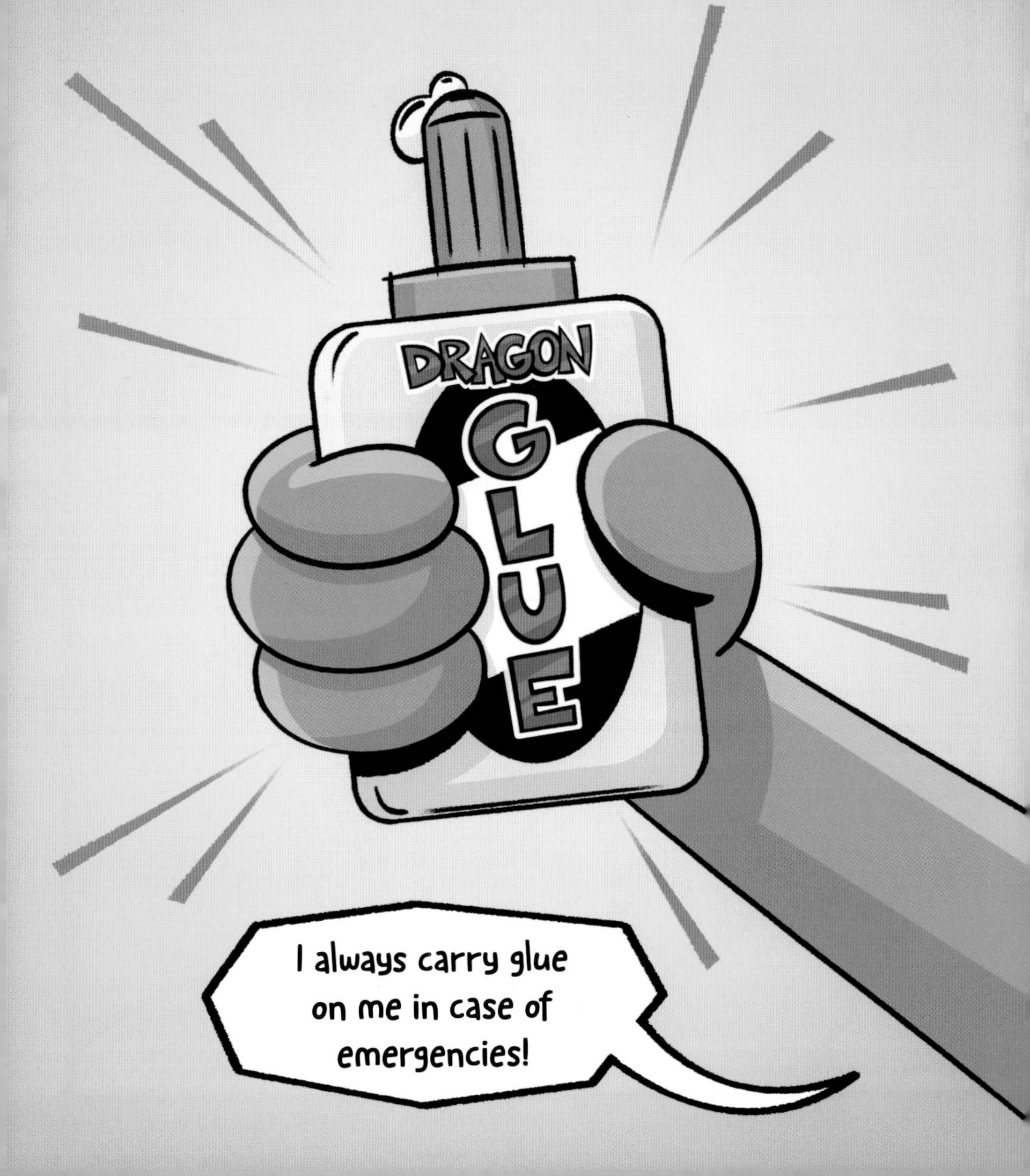
DRAGON GLUE
I always carry glue on me in case of emergencies!

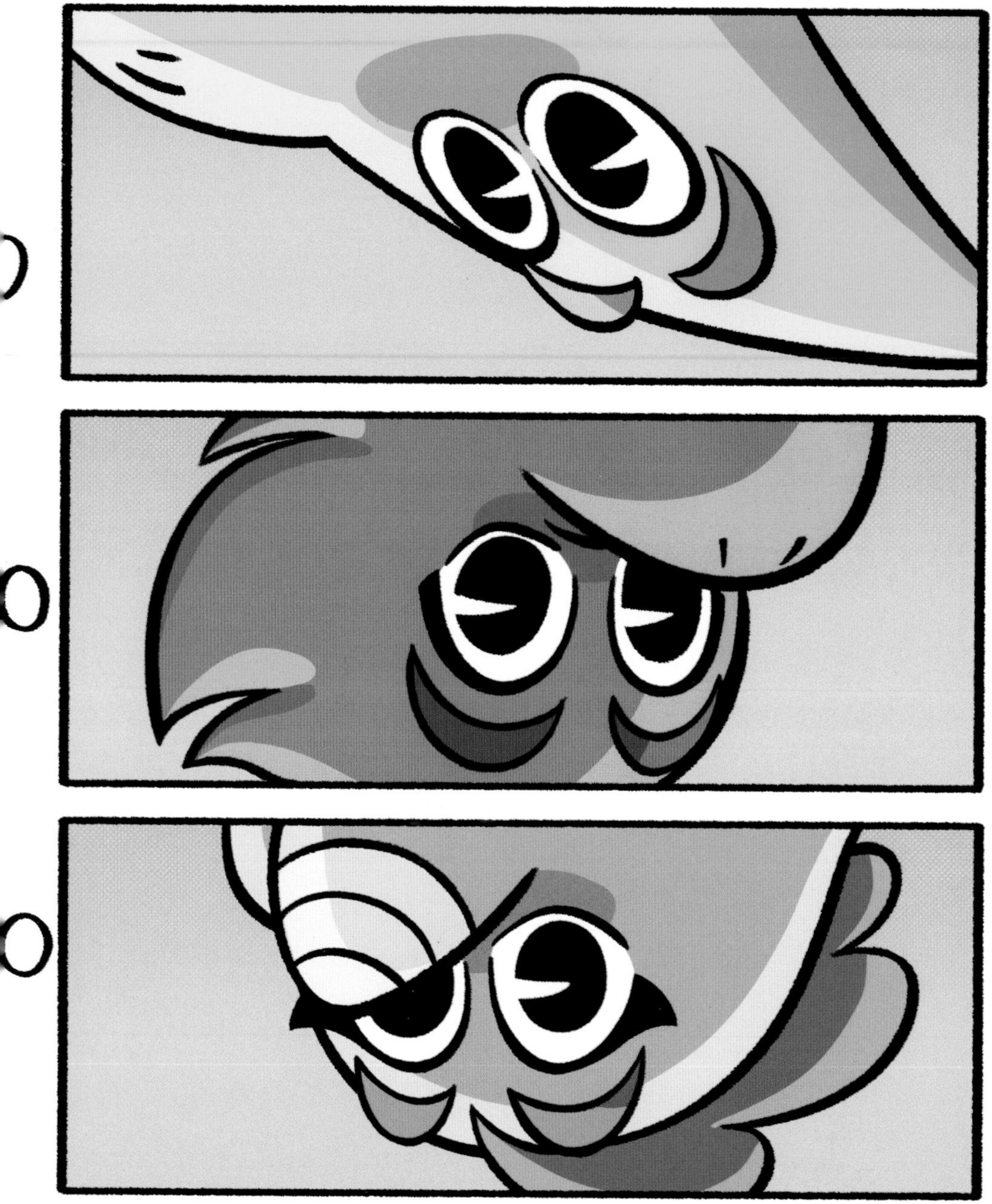

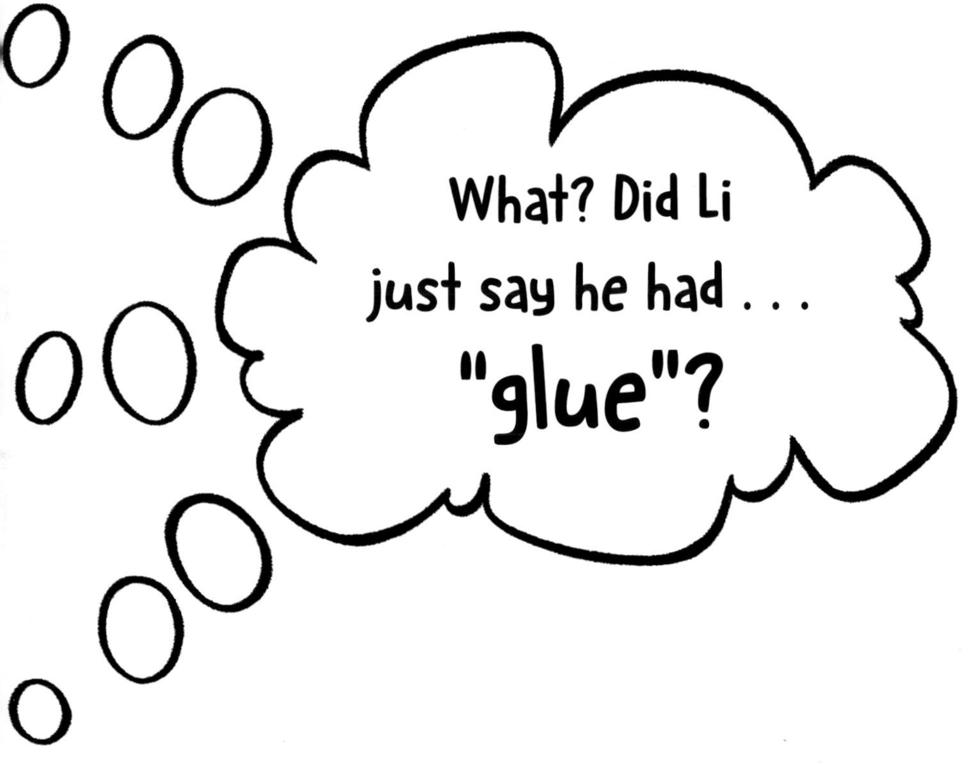
What? Did Li
just say he had . . .
"glue"?

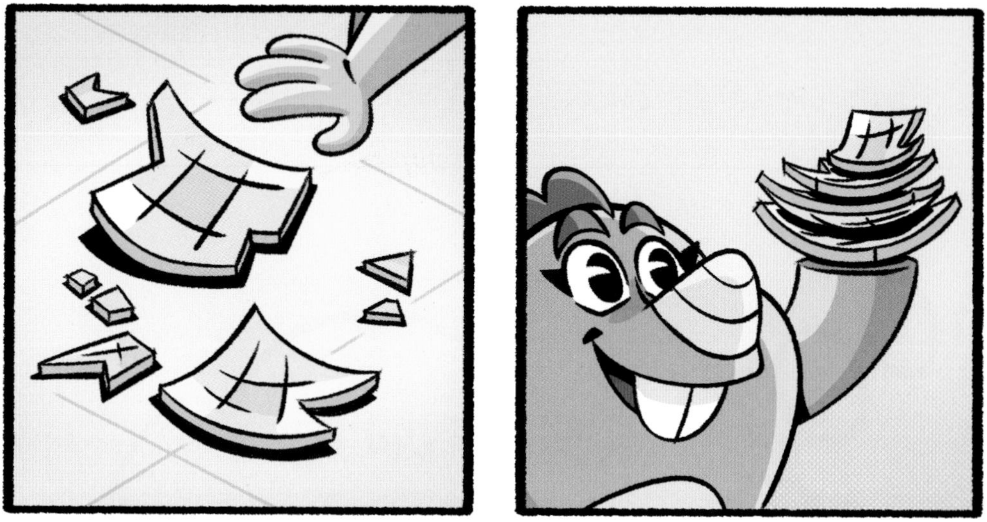

Runa and Fizz gathered up the scattered pieces of the disco ball.

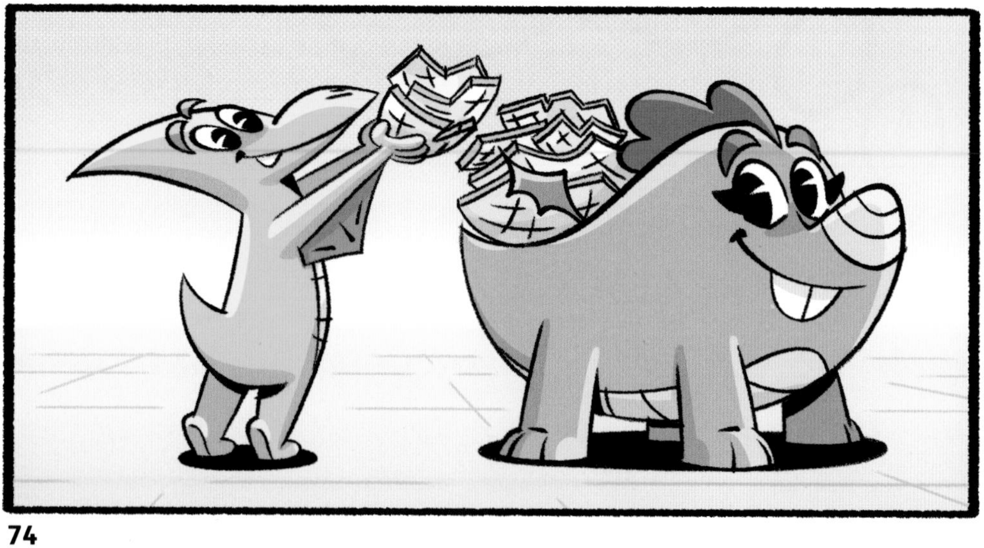

Drake and Li stuck each piece back
together one by one.

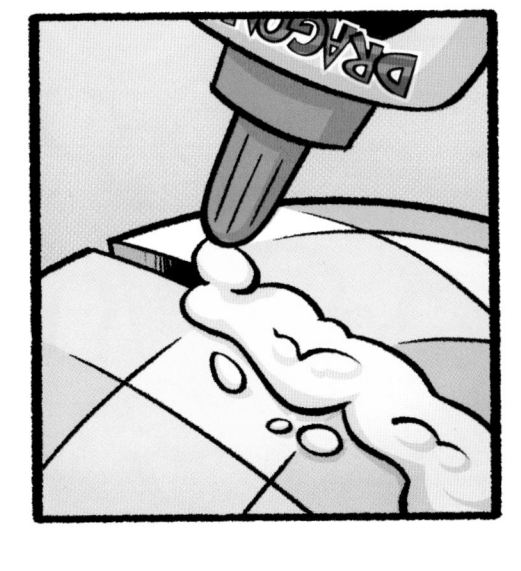

The disco ball was whole again, but it looked like it was still missing something. . . . Something magical.

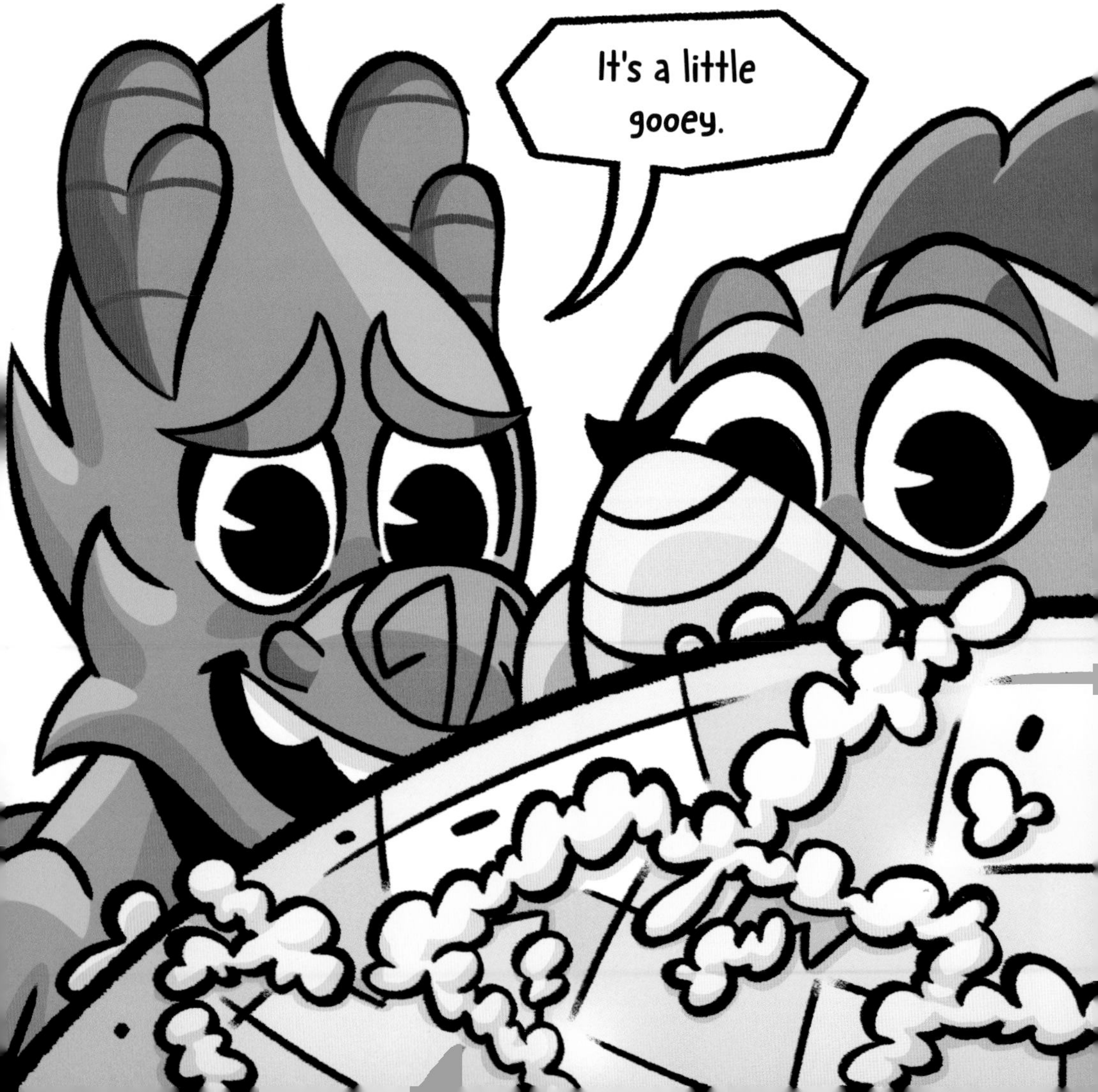
It's a little gooey.

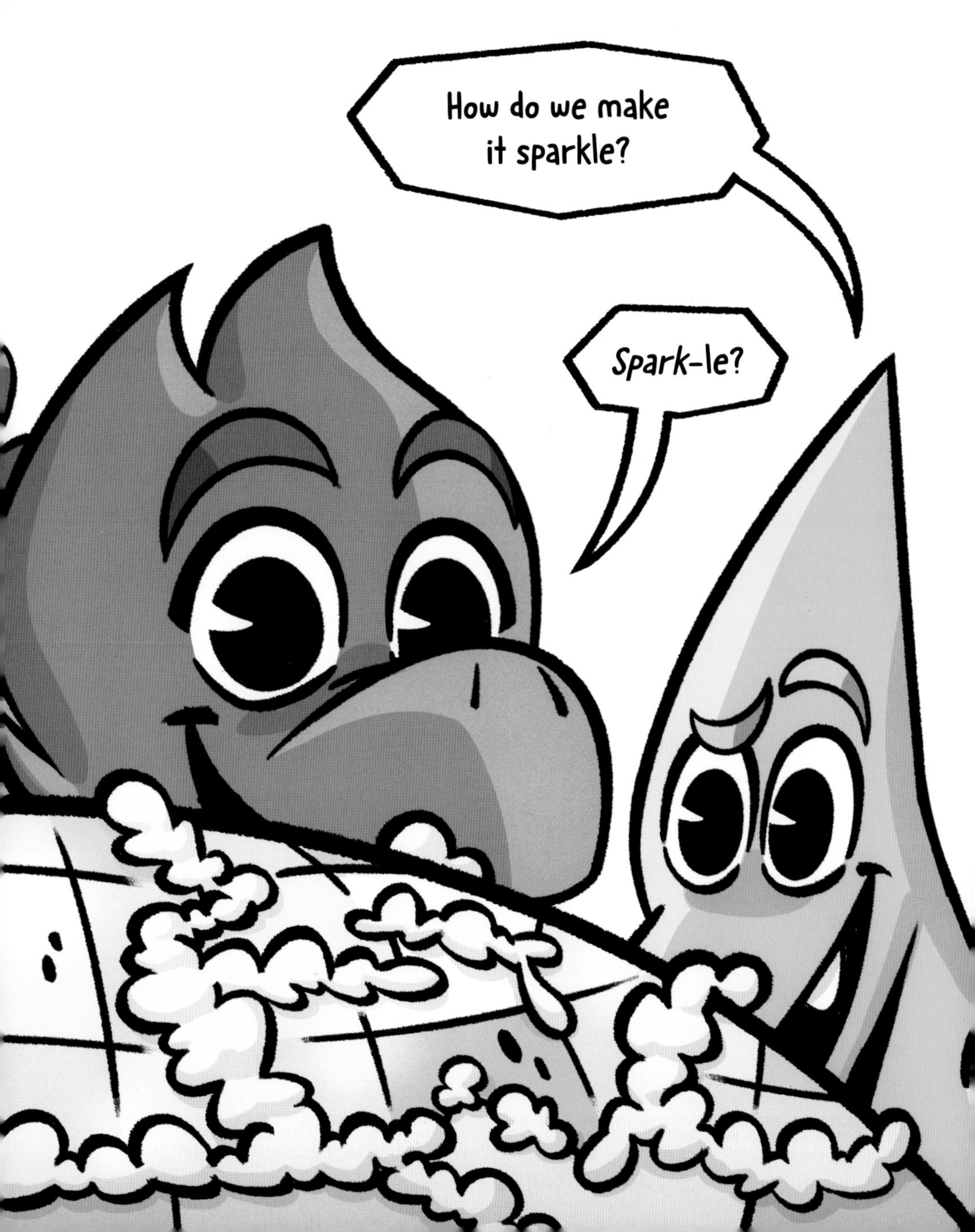
How do we make it sparkle?
Spark-le?

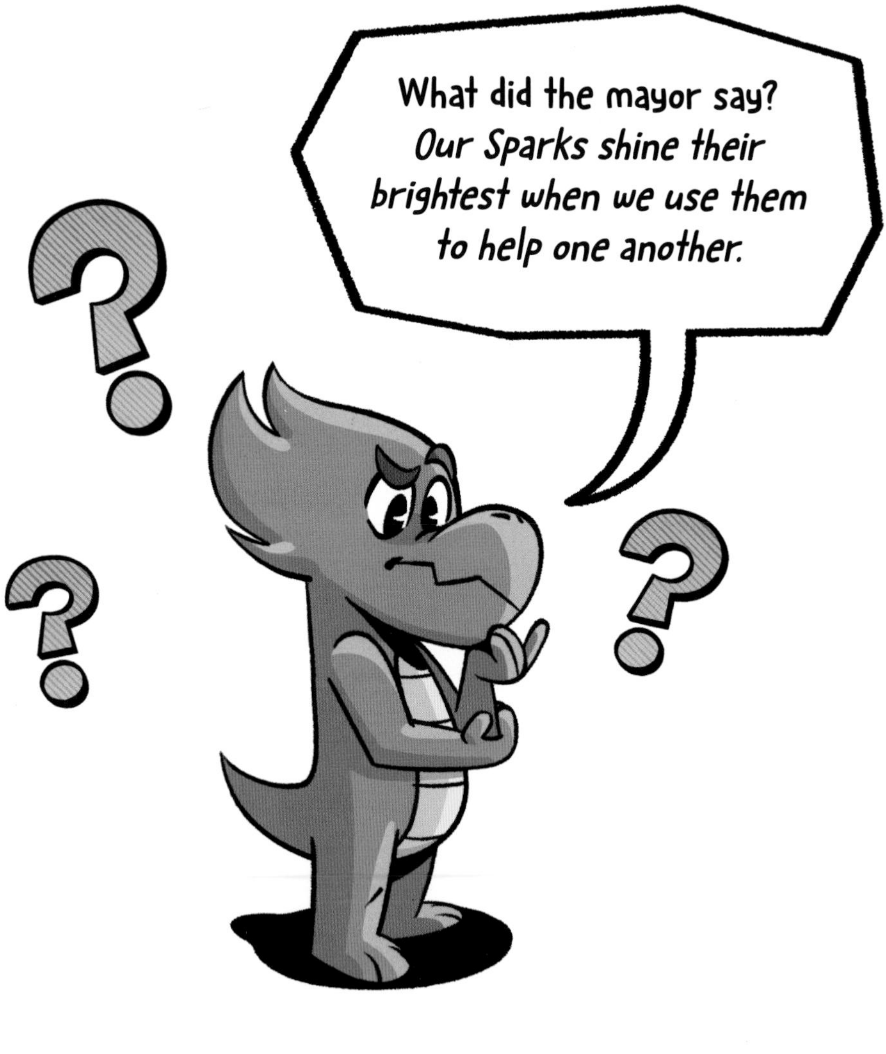
What did the mayor say?
Our Sparks shine their brightest when we use them to help one another.

Drake remembered the story of the dragons on the first Spark Day and how the disco ball received its glow.

It wasn't just *one* dragon's Spark that lit the disco ball, but the Sparks of *all* the dragons that made such a special light!

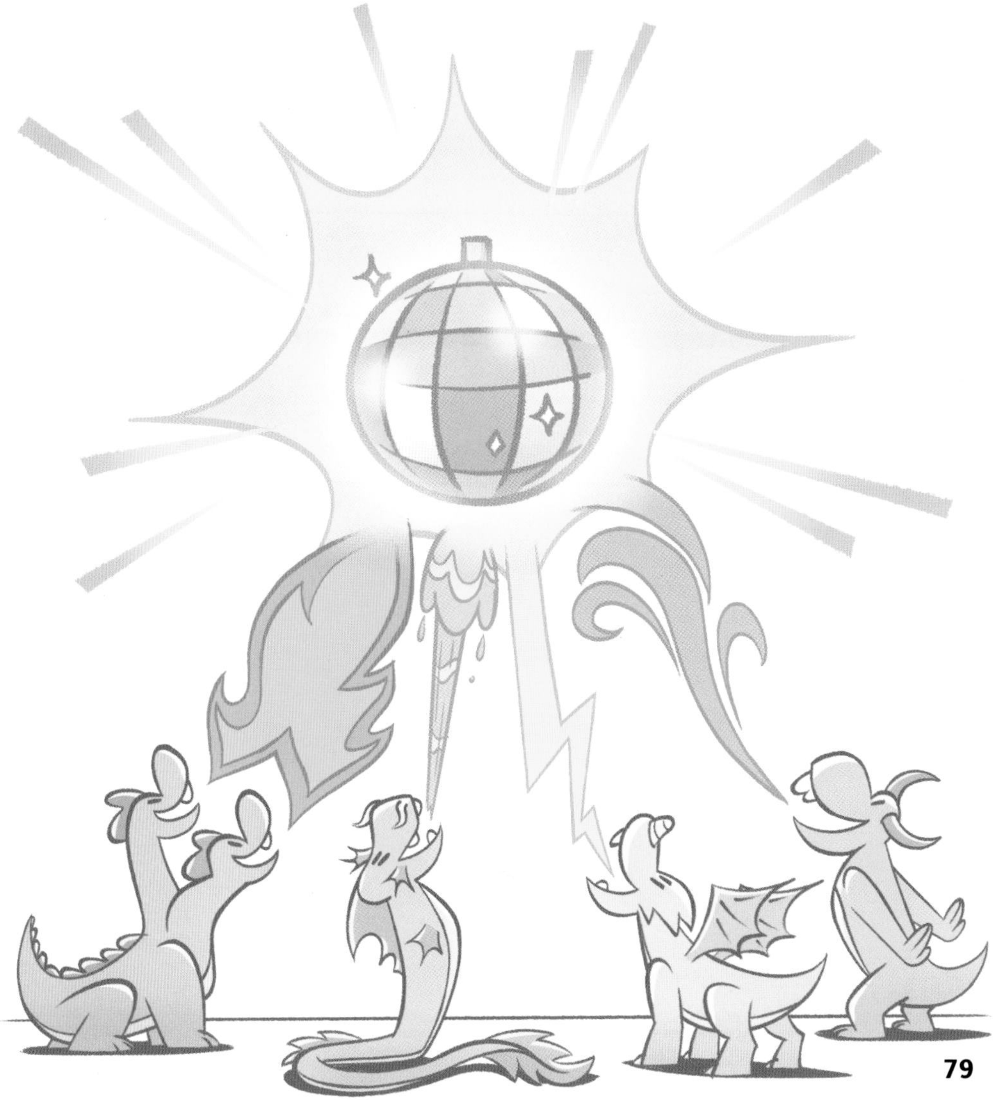

That was it! They all knew what they had to do: use the power of their Sparks to help one another!

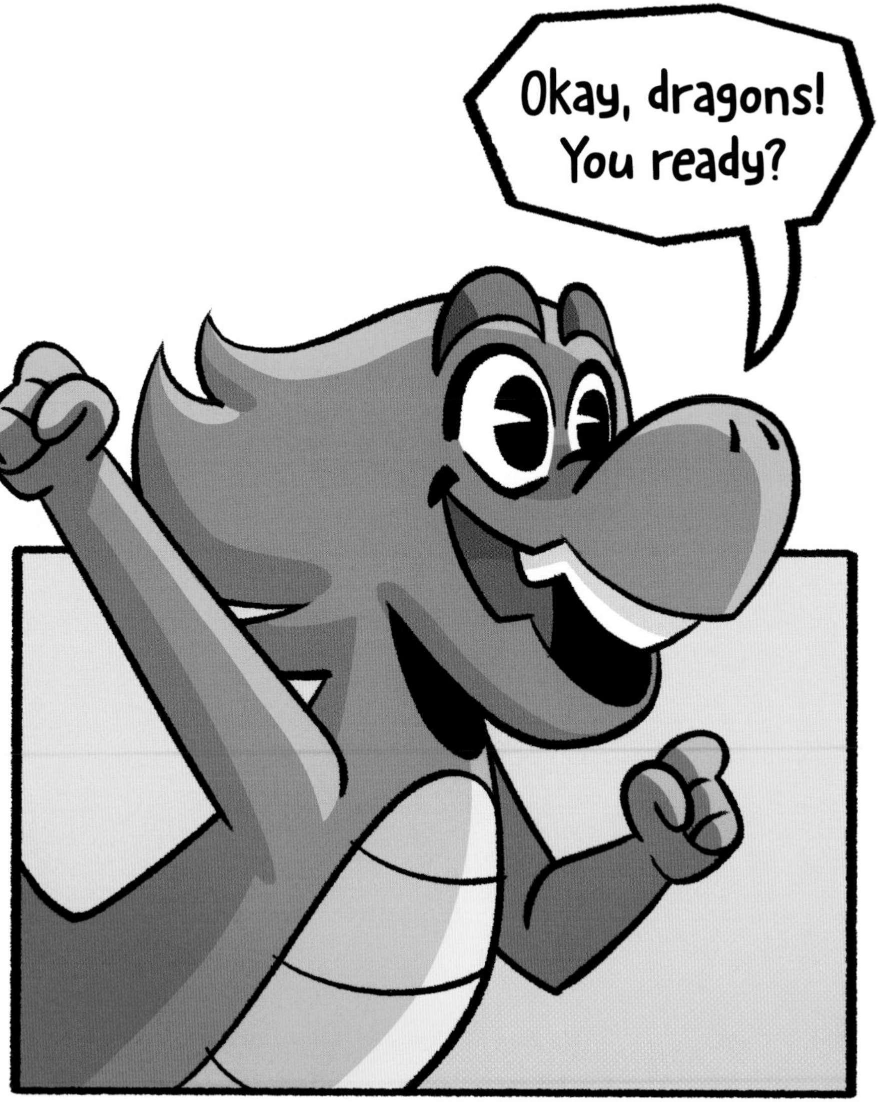
Okay, dragons! You ready?

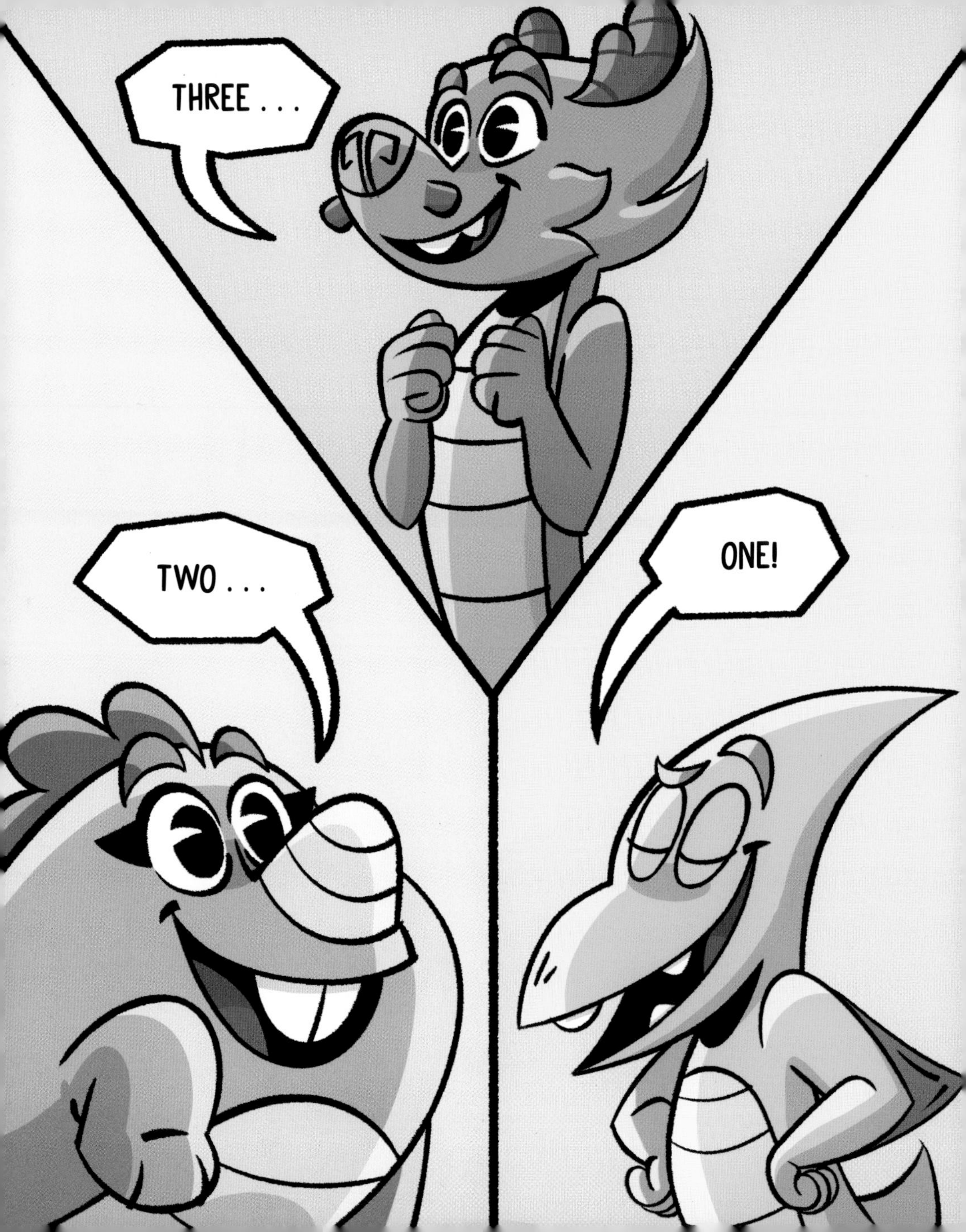
THREE . . .
TWO . . .
ONE!

Together they used their Sparks on
the disco ball. . . .

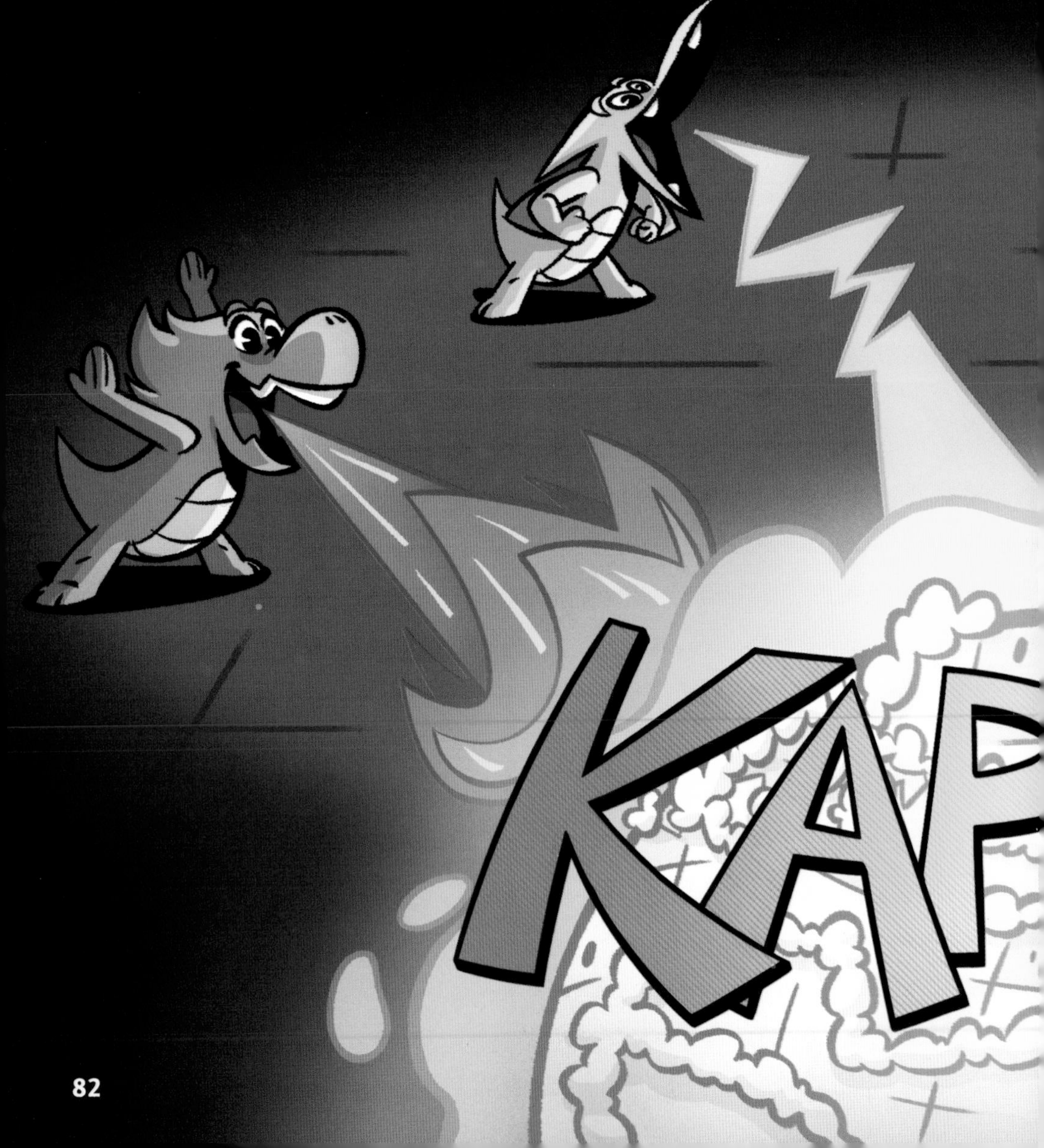
KAP

And something magical happened!

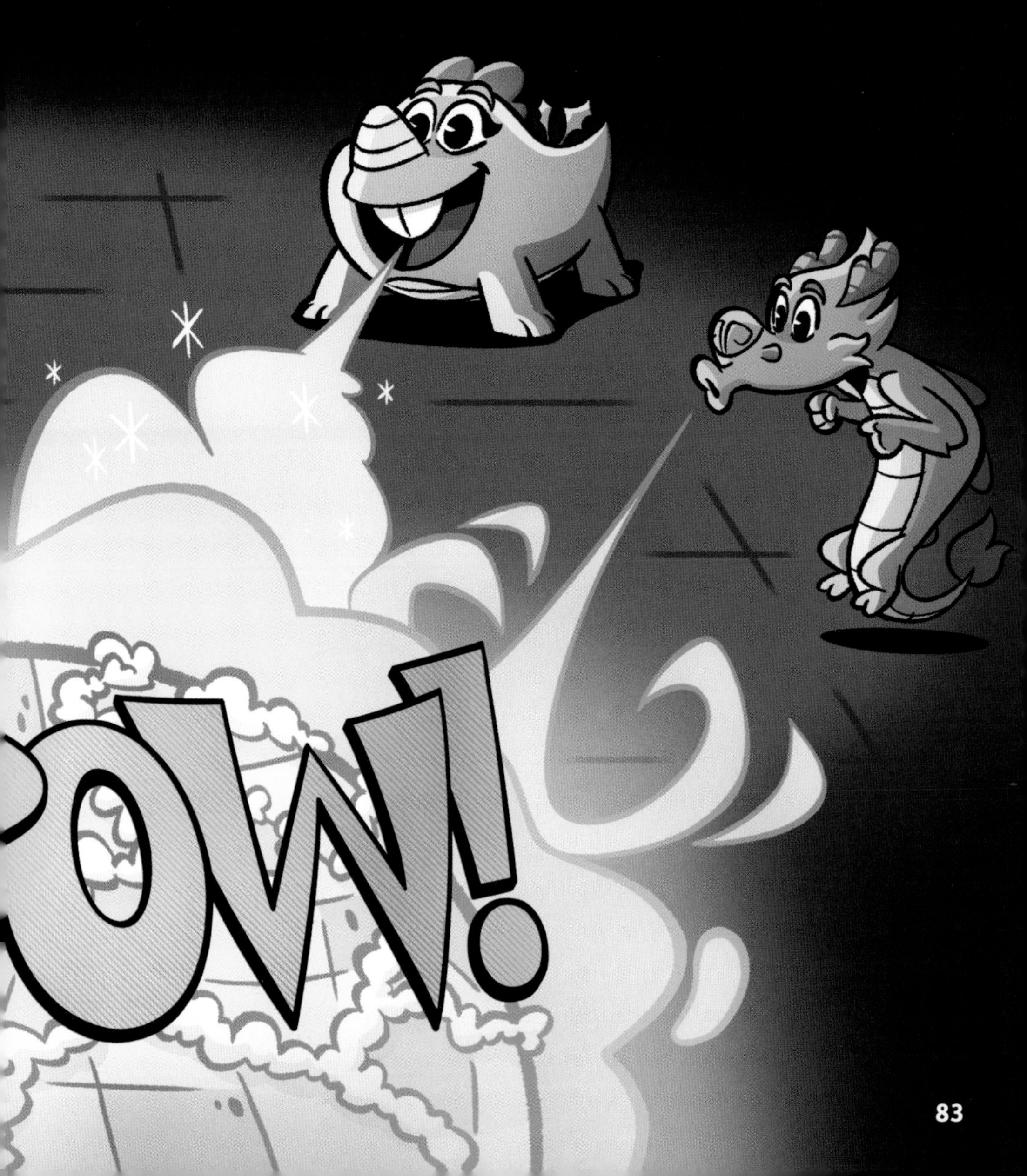
OW!

The disco ball glowed brightly, the light of their shared Sparks illuminating Ember City's sky in a dazzling display.

Every dragon across the land saw the light and knew . . .

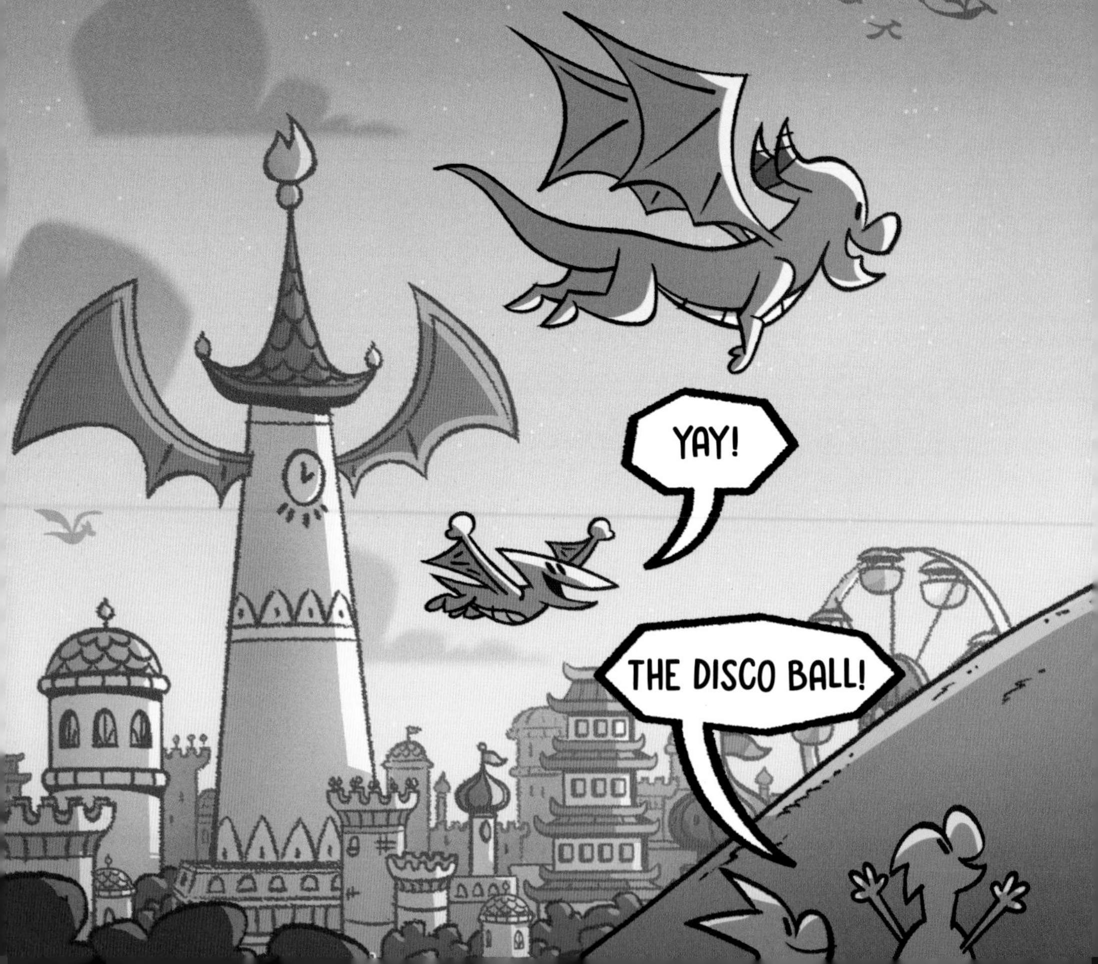
YAY!
THE DISCO BALL!

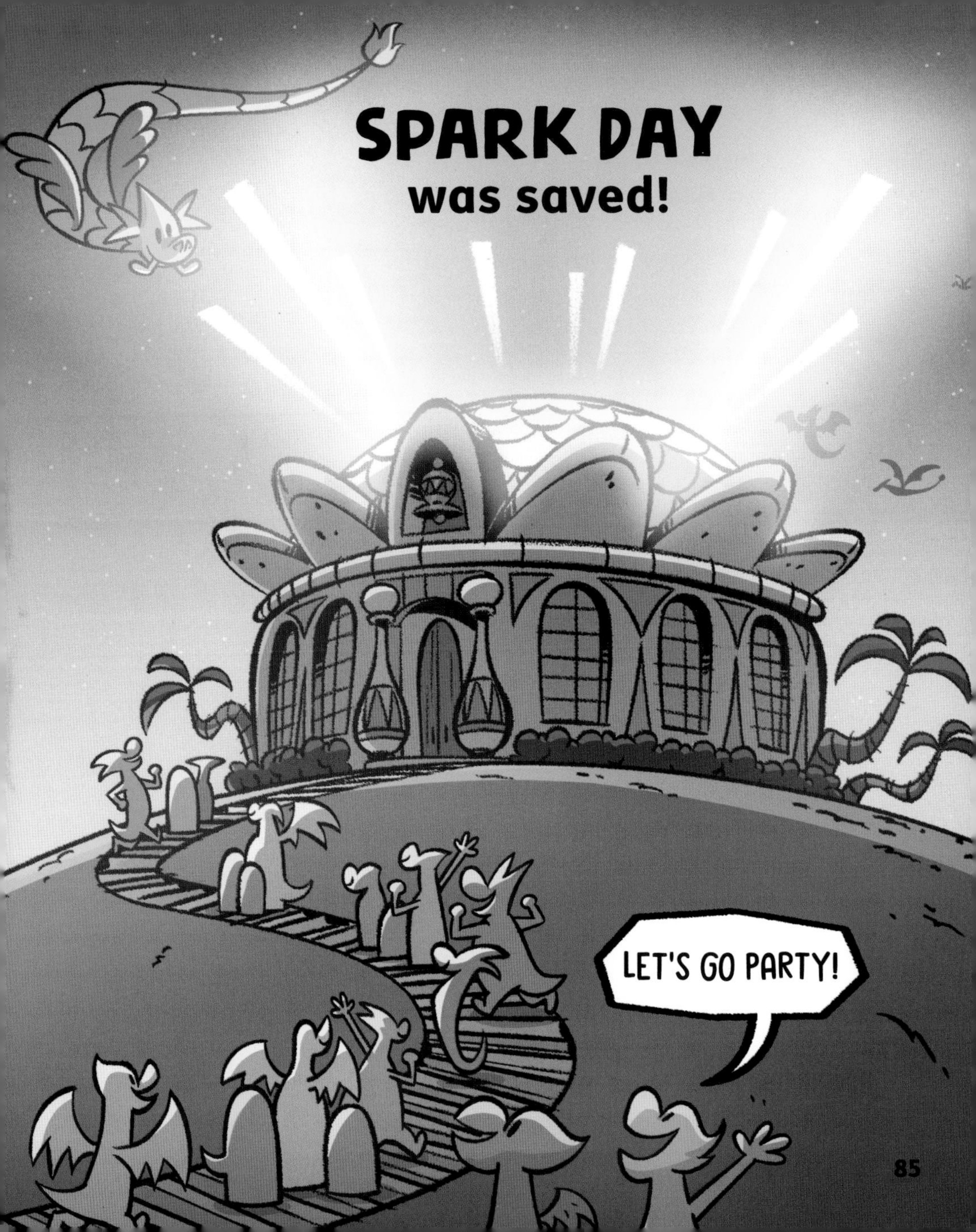
SPARK DAY
was saved!
LET'S GO PARTY!

CHAPTER SIX

The new disco ball floated up above
Drake, Runa, Li, and Fizz.

They had never seen a more
beautiful sight.

Their Sparks lit up the disco ball like
a rainbow, shining colors everywhere.

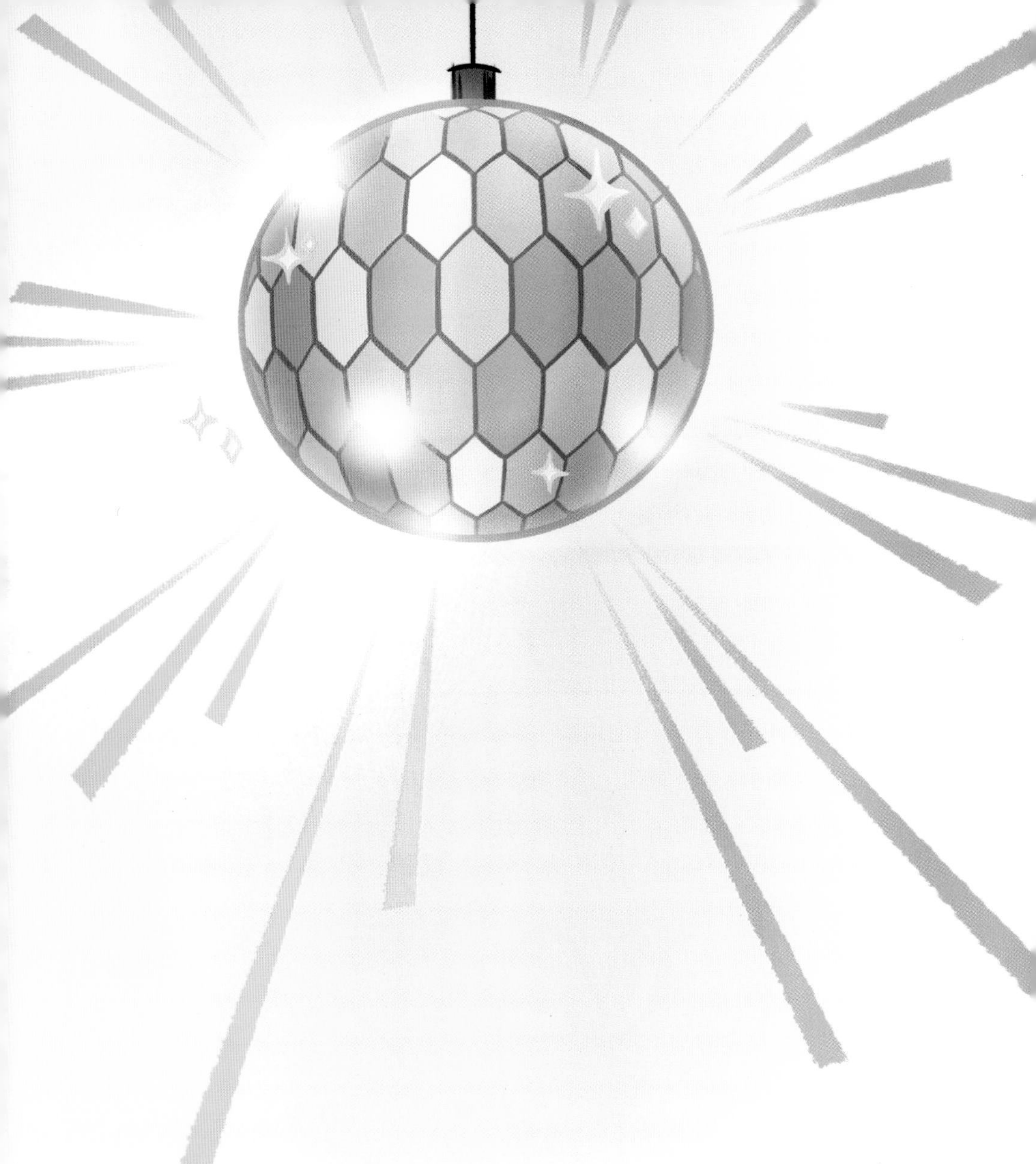

Mayor Copper returned to the party with the rest of the dragons of Ember City.

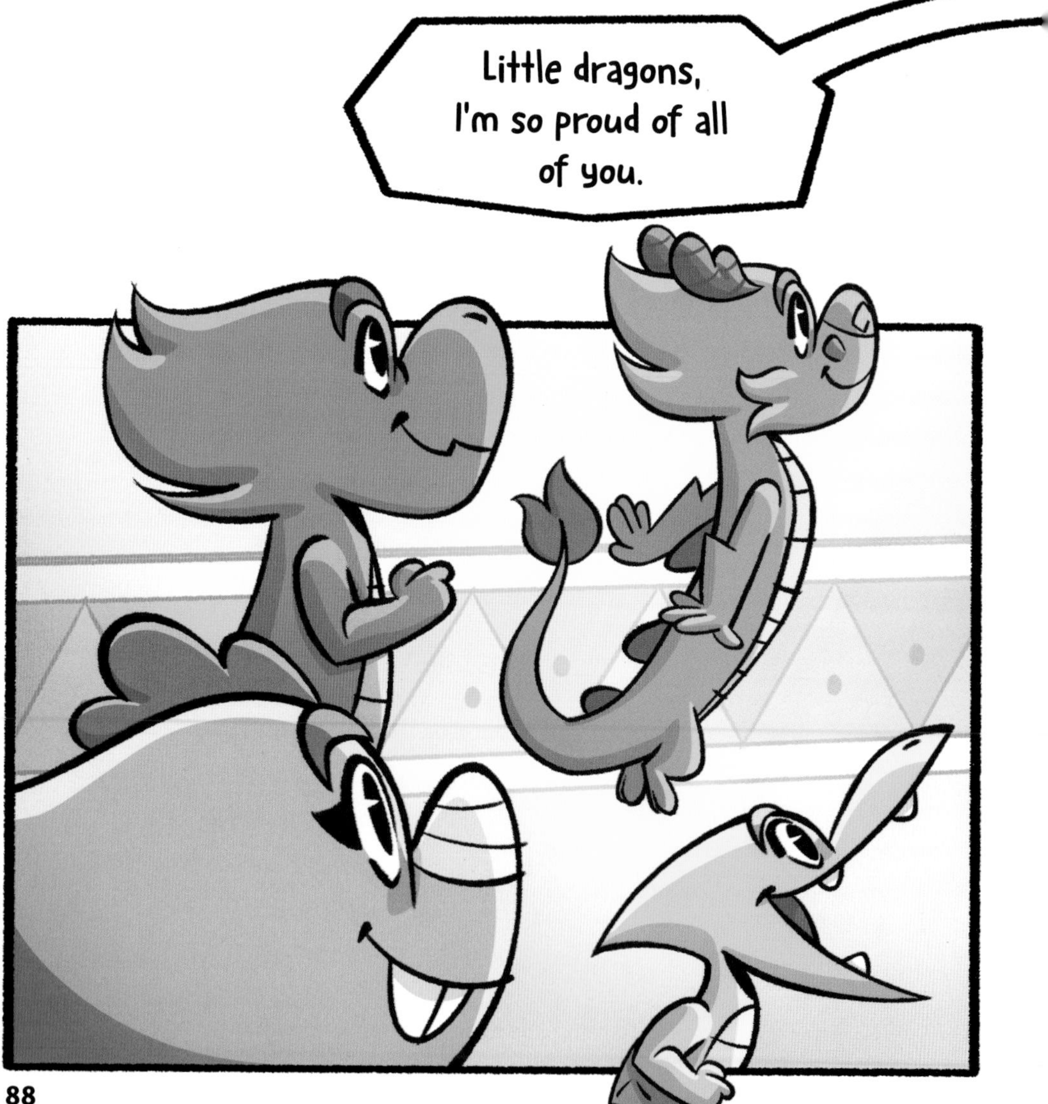
Little dragons, I'm so proud of all of you.

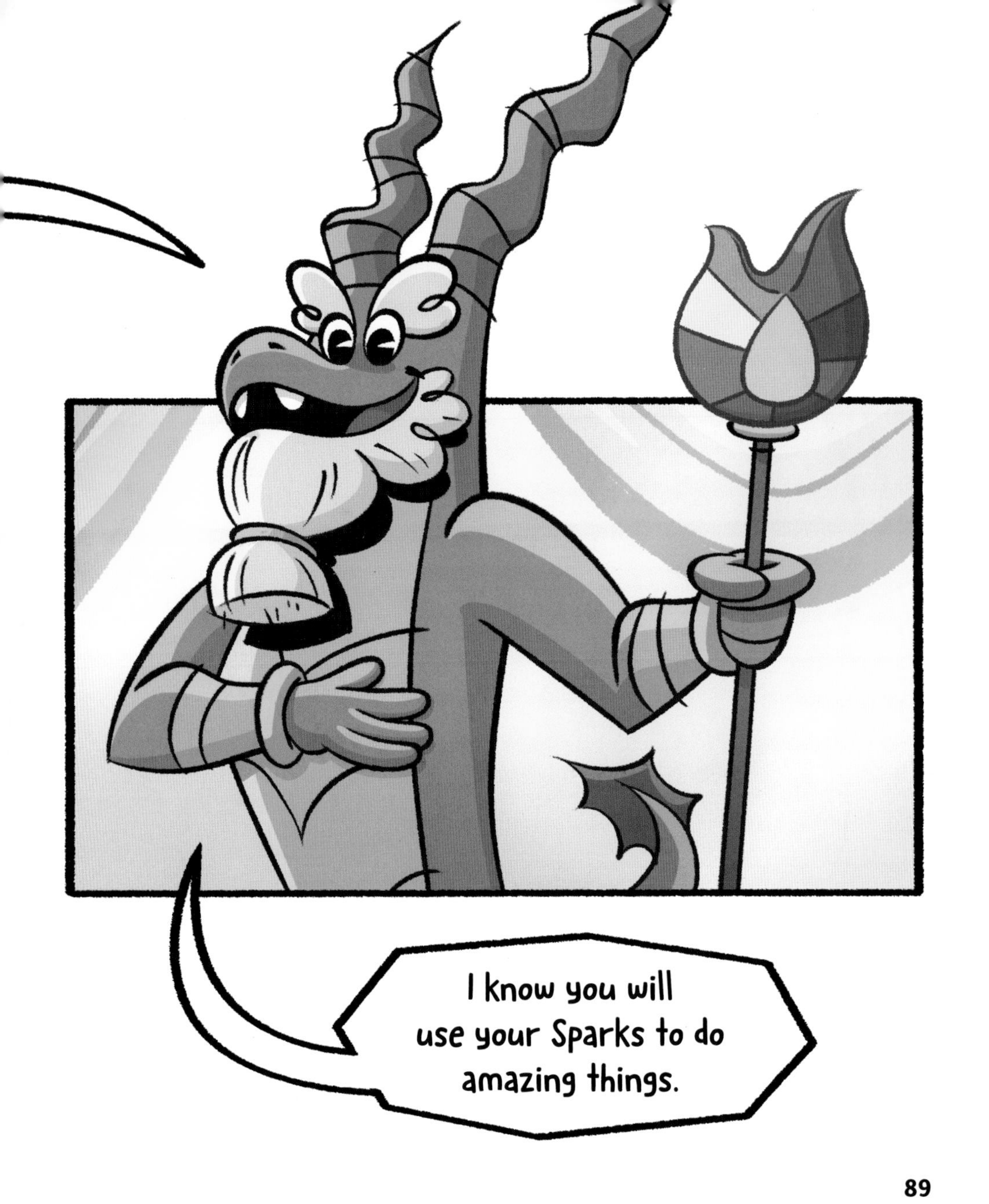
I know you will use your Sparks to do amazing things.

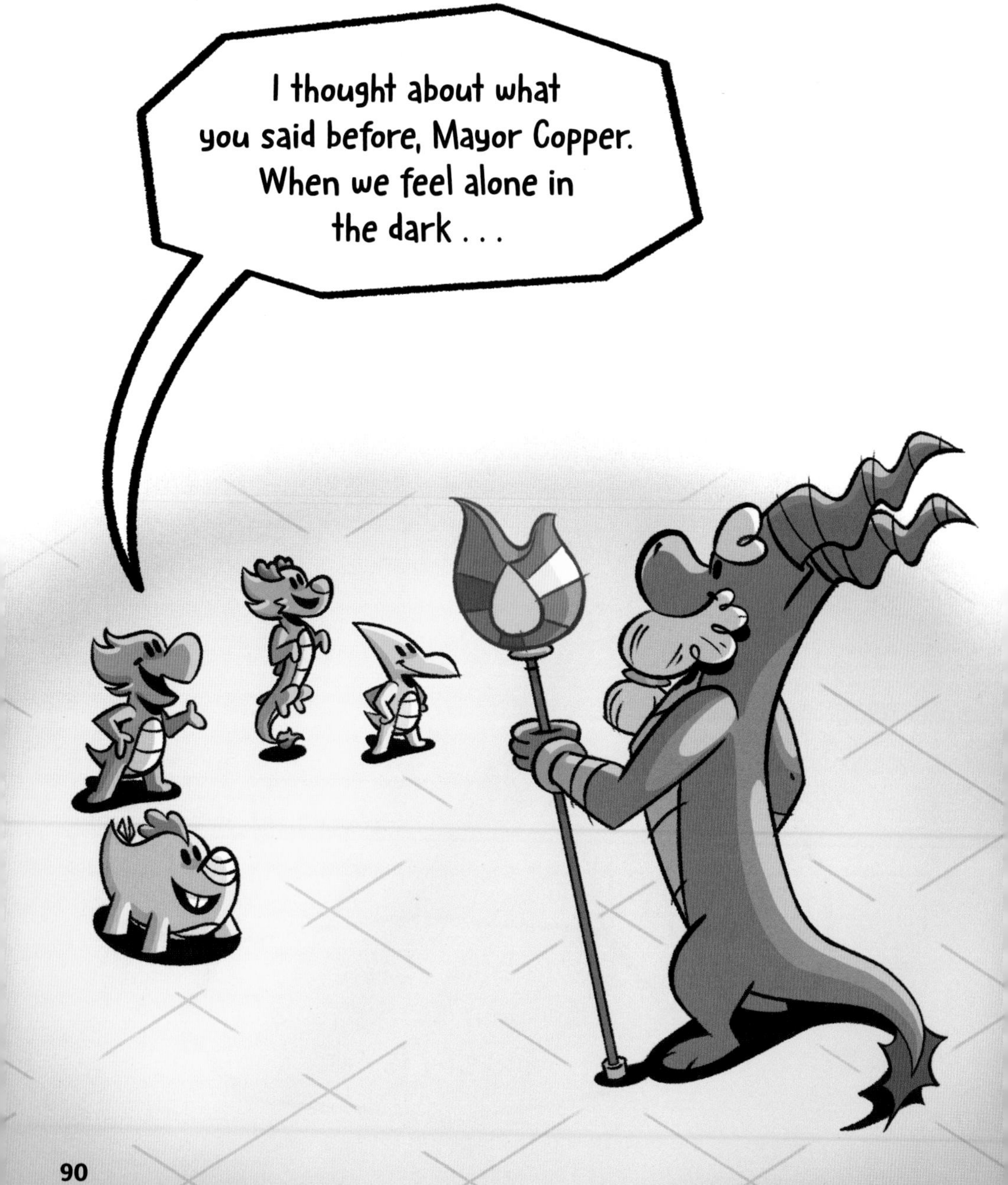
I thought about what you said before, Mayor Copper. When we feel alone in the dark . . .

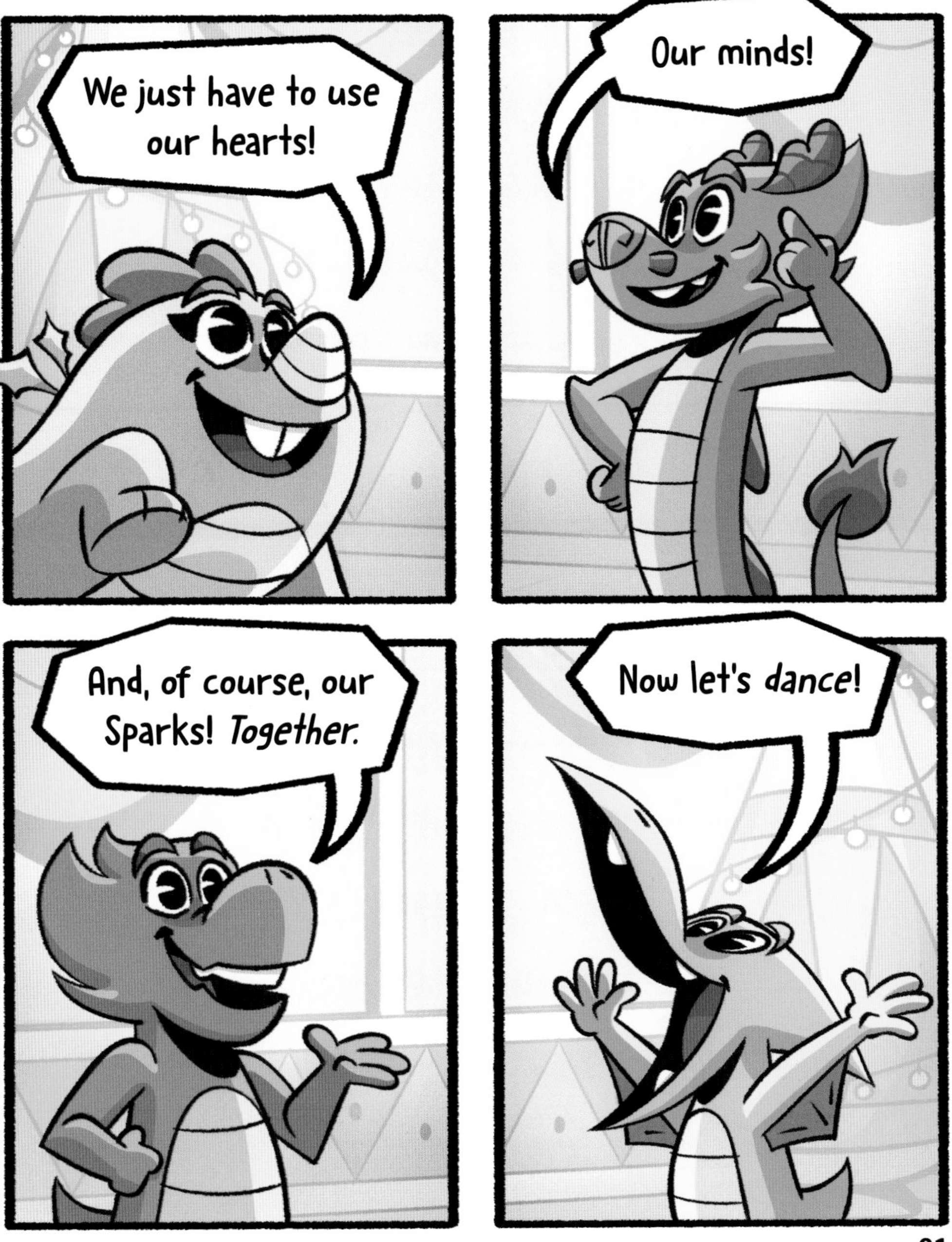
We just have to use our hearts!
Our minds!
And, of course, our Sparks! *Together.*
Now let's *dance*!

Drake, Runa, Li, Fizz, and the other dragons of Ember City danced under the shining light of the new Spark Day disco ball.

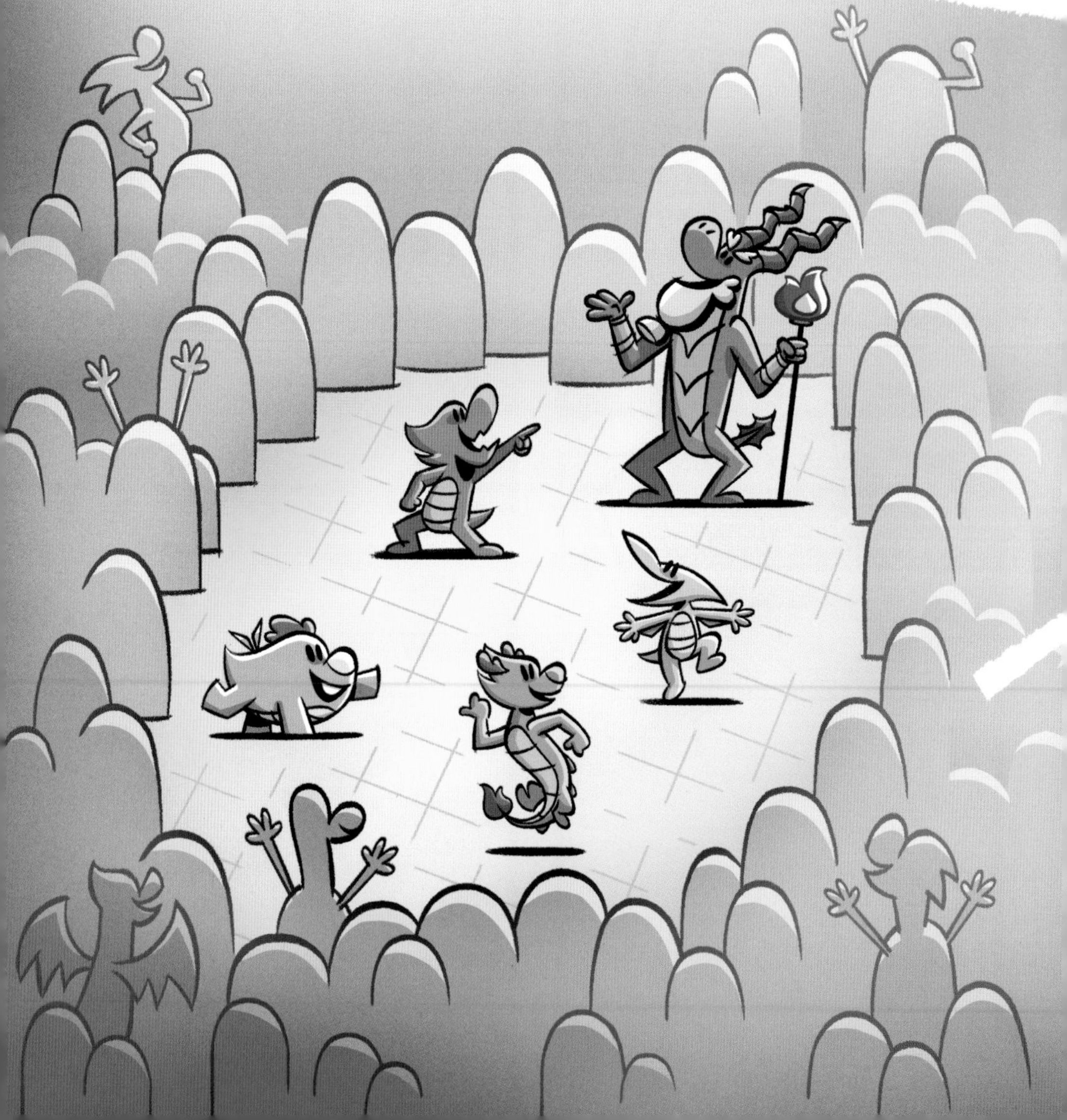

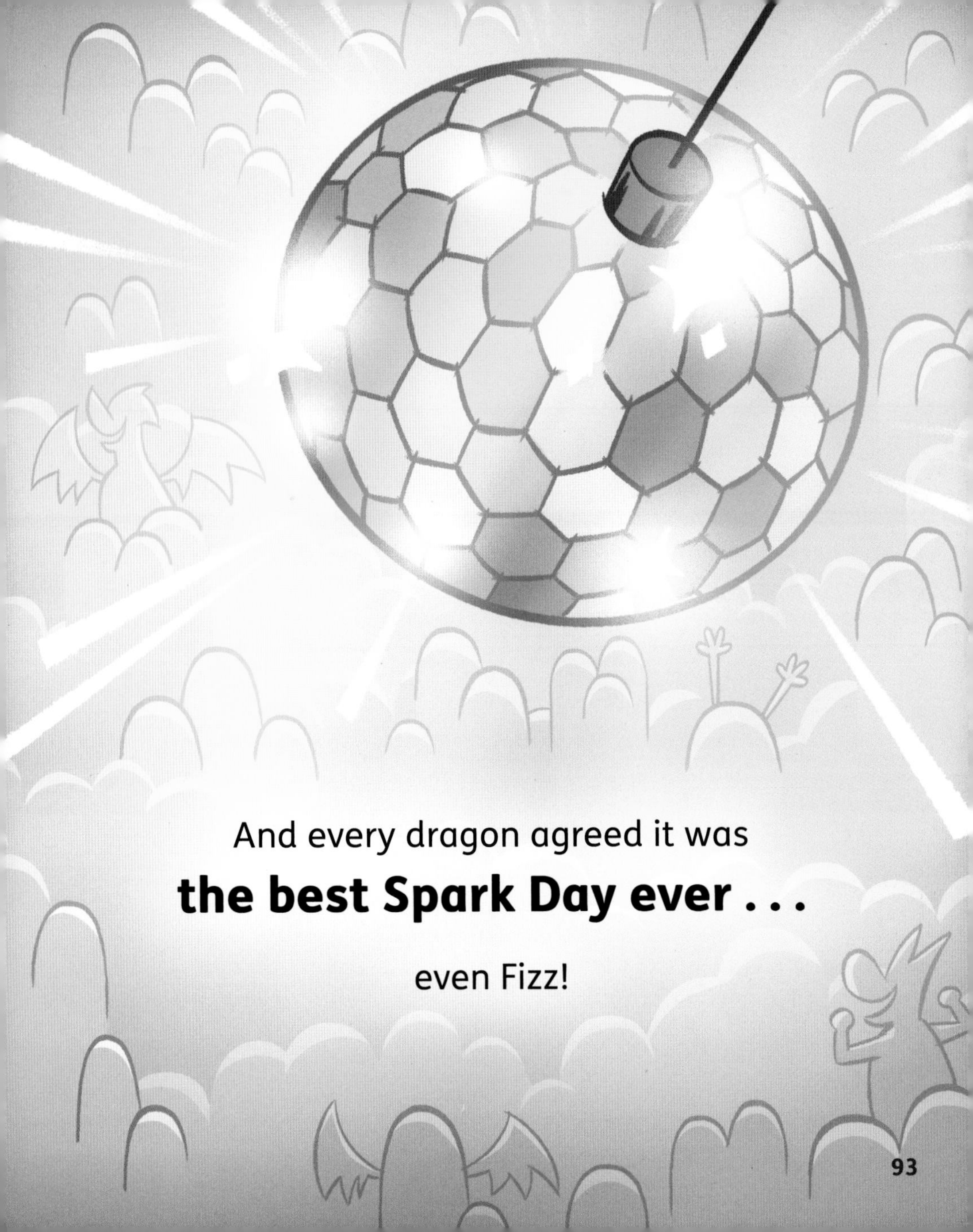

And every dragon agreed it was

the best Spark Day ever . . .

even Fizz!

SHANE RICHARDSON is an author, illustrator, and art director in the animation industry. He has contributed to several animated TV series and films, including *The Casagrandes*, *Santiago of the Seas*, *Shimmer and Shine*, and *The Book of Life*. He lives in Los Angeles, California, with Sarah and their dog, Oliver.

SARAH MARINO is an author, illustrator, and art director in the animation industry. She has contributed to several animated TV series and films, including *Shimmer and Shine*, *Butterbean's Café*, and *The Book of Life*. She lives in Los Angeles, California, with Shane and their dog, Oliver.